Sarah, Mother of Nations

Angelique Conger

Southwest of Zion Publishing

Copyright © 2023 by Angelique Conger

All rights reserved.

No portion of this book may be reproduced in any form without written permission from the publisher or author, except as permitted by U.S. copyright law.

For women who struggle to have children in this life, or who never have this blessing, remember —
All things are possible!

Contents

1. Sacrifice — 1
2. Freedom — 11
3. Escape — 18
4. Rose and Thorn — 29
5. Harran — 39
6. Thieves — 47
7. Traitor — 57
8. Sorrow — 67
9. Damascus — 76
10. Drought — 84
11. Abram's Sister — 94
12. Hagar — 103
13. Women's Court — 115
14. Leaving Egypt — 125
15. Battle of Giants — 134
16. Choice — 142
17. Answers — 149
18. Concubine — 154
19. New Names — 164

20.	Blessing	173
21.	Nothing is Impossible	180
22.	Banished	189
23.	Treaty	196
24.	Another Sacrifice	202

Afterword	210
Acknowledgements	211
Also By Angelique Conger	213
About the Author	215

Chapter One

Sacrifice

The frightened cry of the child filled the temple square as the priest lifted it into the air above the altar. The mother's grief-stricken shriek echoed dissonantly through the enclosed court surrounding the temple. The screams ceased, like a suddenly closing heavy door blocking all sound. The priest's black obsidian knife slashed across the child's chest and its cry ended, followed by the rejoicing shouts from the crowd. Blood dripped from his hands onto his black kirtle.

My blood ran cold. I hated the bloody sacrifices to Elkenah that the leadership of Ur forced us to watch. Why would the priests sacrifice innocent children? What god would accept a child as a thank offering?

I clung to Abram's arm and fought back the tears. *That child could have been ours. I would eagerly take it, boy or girl.* My arms felt empty and cold. Could I survive this if that child were mine?

Other priests dressed in similar robes to the high priest dragged a young woman toward the same altar, her body displayed for all to see through her sheer white garment.

Abram hissed. "Not Hathor."

"Hathor is as innocent as the child," I gasped.

"And one of the few who follow Jehovah here in Ur." Abram's whispering voice scratched my ear.

The priest lay her on the altar looking much like a hard bed, with tall curved ends at the head and foot. Hathor fought to escape, kicking and screaming, as they tied her to the altar. Her screams became prayers to Jehovah until the cheering crowd overwhelmed them. I closed my eyes, trying not to listen.

"This virgin refuses to participate in the temple or rites of Elkenah or any of the other gods of Ur," the priest said. The shape at the top of the space focused his voice and overrode the noise of the crowd. "She refuses to become a priestess to Elkenah. We must sacrifice her to atone for her sin."

Jeers erupted from the crowd, chilling me.

Even with my eyes closed tight, I could sense when the hand gripping the bloody knife rose high into the air, as the crowd inhaled as one. Then they cheered. *He must have lifted Hathor's still beating heart.* I could not look.

Tears flowed into Abram's sleeve where I had buried my face. My trembling fingertips touched my mouth. I swallowed rapidly, again and again.

"Is it ... Is it over?" I mewled, my voice drying up mid-sentence. *How could they do this to an innocent woman?*

"No!"

Abram's cry forced my head from his shoulder. I took a shaky breath as I gawped up the many steps leading to the altar. Priests dragged two more young women upward, dressed like the first in the sheer white of Elkenah's priestesses.

"How can they do this?" I cried. I cringed and rubbed my palm against my heart. Hathor, Onofria, and Ain were the royal daughters of Onitah. They descend directly from Ham.

"And they are followers of Jehovah," Abram murmured. His hands scrubbed against his robes.

I could barely hear him through the roar of my beating heart and the barrage of mockery coming from the crowd. Their words made me want to clap my hands over my ears, but I could not. It would draw attention to us.

"Atone for your sins!"

"Bow down to Elkenah!"

"Worship Shagreel, the sun!"

"You should have offered your worship to Libnah!"

"They worship Jehovah," I breathed into Abram's ear. My stomach churned at the thought. *If they know those women worship Jehovah, did they know about me and Abram? Will we be next? How did they learn of the women Abram recently taught of Jehovah?* I swallowed back the burn of bile in the back of my throat. The stench of death mingled with the fetid reek of the onlookers' sweat, lust, and excitement.

"Stay calm, Sarai," Abram's words warmed my ear.

I nodded, trying to mask my shuddering body.

"These two virgins, sisters of the first, also refuse to honor our gods. They refuse to mate with the priests, reject our offer to become priestesses, and will not bow before the gods."

Shouts filled the square.

My heart thudded in my chest as the words "sacrifice them" echoed louder than any other words.

The women fought to escape the priests. Ain, smaller than her remaining sister, ducked under the arms of the priest who held her, freeing herself. With her dark hair flowing down her back, she raced down the steps. The onlookers seemed to hold their breath. In the sudden near silence, I could hear her crying for help, begging someone to help her or hide her. But what could I do? I could not overwhelm the priests.

Men from the crowd ran up the stairs toward Ain. She begged them to help her escape, grasping their hands as tears flowed down her face. Instead, they wrenched her arms behind her back and forced her to climb the steps into the waiting arms of the priests.

Cheers filled the square, ending the unnatural calm. I quivered and shuffled my feet back, wanting to turn and flee. Abram held my hand, pinning me to his side. "Remember, it is the law. We must watch," he whispered.

Tall, dark Onofria vainly struggled against the powerful arms of the priest who held her.

"You will watch your sister die, then you, too, will give yourself to Elkenah." The priest called loud enough for all to hear.

The other priests pushed the kicking, hitting, and biting Ain to the altar and tied her to it. She screamed her defiance. "No god of wood or stone will receive my prayers!"

The black and crimson-stained knife rose into the air, and I squeezed my eyes as firmly closed as I could, sickened by the exaltations of the crowd. I waited for the noise of the crowd's celebration to wane before opening them once more.

I gasped as the jubilant crowd thundered when the high priest rolled Ain's limp body off the altar. Another priest took a foot and dragged her body away. I fought back a gag.

Onofria walked serenely toward the altar, her lips moving in silent prayer.

"You pray to Elkenah now?" the priest mocked. "When it is too late to save you? Elkenah will not forgive you."

The crowd stilled, listening for her answer. I held my breath.

"I pray to my God," Onofria said, sitting on the edge of the altar. "You need not tie me, for I will not fight. Jehovah will take me into his loving arms." She lay in her sisters' blood on the altar bed.

The priest sneered, "Your Jehovah will not save you."

"It matters not," Onofria said.

I took a slow, shaky breath at her bravery. *Could I show such bravery?*

Her regal manner silenced the jeers coming from the crowd.

Even I watched in awe, grimacing and wanting to look away, as the black knife fell toward Onofria's heart.

The priest lifted the still beating heart from Onofria's body. "Jehovah is no better than Elkenah. He did not protect this woman."

The mass of people in the square howled their agreement.

"She trusted Jehovah," I whispered. "Why did He not save her?"

"We cannot know His will," Abram replied in a low whisper, his shoulders sagging. "He took them from this wicked world. The blood of these innocents will cry for vengeance."

The mob cheered and hooted, demanding another offering to Elkenah. Their blood lust removed any sense of care for the victims.

At a word from the high priest, the other priests ran down the steps into the screeching crowd, searching for another victim. Abram and I mingled in the crowd, pretending to shout and raising our fists like the others, but making no noise. I wanted to run away, but we remained still within the screaming mob, trying not to be seen.

The priests spread out, pushing and shoving through the crowd, seeking someone specific.

I clenched my jaw and wanted to fight the closing crowd off as three big priests came toward us. I prayed they would go another way, find another to sacrifice. But their eyes focused on Abram. I gasped.

Abram took my arm and stepped backward behind two big men, holding me close. It did not help, for the priests pushed them aside.

"You!" one shouted, pointing at Abram.

"Me?" Abram almost squeaked, pointing to his chest. He turned his head from side to side, his eyes wide open.

"You refuse to bow down to the gods of Ur. I know you as a follower of Jehovah. You are next to be sacrificed."

I stepped backward. Abram resolutely grasped my arm. "Run."

We tried to escape them. But the throng of worshipers surrounded us, crowding us into the center of a knot of the screaming multitude, not giving us space to break away.

My heart beat wildly as I elbowed the men encircling me. I looked for a small space to duck away from the crowd. None appeared. My skin felt clammy. They had us trapped.

Only when the priests shouted commands to let them through did a man who had trapped us step back. A priest reached forward and grabbed the front of Abram's tunic.

"Run, Sarai!" Abram cried.

I screamed and fell to the ground, landing on my knees. The men surrounding me stepped back as I scooted between their legs and ran from them, slowing only when no one's hands tried to slow me.

Abram! What will I do without you? Jehovah, protect him! My tongue stuck to the top of my mouth. I searched everywhere for an escape route.

At the edge of the crowd, near the court wall, I stopped to look back. I had to know what would happen to my beloved husband.

Unwilling to race away from Abram's plight, I turned back near the entrance to scowl at the temple altar. Black clad priests dragged Abram up the steep stairs toward the bloody altar.

Abram had stopped fighting, but he had lost his footing, slipping against a priest, knocking them both over. The men dragged him backward up the stairs. His feet bounced beneath him.

I put my fist into my mouth and whimpered, unwilling to allow the jeering mob to hear my screams. *Jehovah, keep Abram safe. Free him from this danger. Keep him safe for me, for you. He loves you and only wants to obey.*

The priests stripped Abram of his tunic and wrestled him to the altar, tying him with double the number of ropes they had used for the young women.

Because of the shape of the top of the altar, I heard Abram's prayers far from the altar at my spot near the edge of the courtyard as he begged Jehovah for help.

The priests stepped back and nodded to the high priest.

No. Do not sacrifice my man!

"This man who believes Jehovah will save him will discover His God is no better than Elkenah," the high priest proclaimed. "You will see when I cut his beating heart from his body."

The crowd roared, seeking to sate their lusts with his blood. I gagged at the stench. *How can these people desire the death of anyone, especially my righteous husband?*

The high priest lifted his black knife.

Unexpectedly, a man dressed in a white robe brighter than the sun appeared beside Abram, silencing the uproar of the mob.

I had heard about these. Abram had taught me what men like this were.

An angel!

"You forgot your God, worshiping the gods of Elkenah, Libnah, and Mahmackrah," the angel said. Although he spoke in a muted voice, it echoed across the square.

The high priest glared at the angel. "Where did you come from?" He motioned to the other priests. "Get him!"

The angel continued. "You have taken the lives of innocent women and children. You now desire to take the life of this righteous man. Jehovah, the God of this earth, is a jealous God. You have been judged guilty."

Priests rushed toward him.

The angel brought his hands together with the sound of thunder, shaking the tall temple building. The priests fell to the floor as the altar crumbled. I shoved a fist into my mouth as Abram crawled from the remains of the altar. He dropped to a crouch on the steps as they swayed and rocked. When the shaking slowed, Abram rushed on down.

Men and women in the square streamed past me, racing to escape the wrath of the angel, no longer chanting for blood. Some fell, their bodies trampled as others hurried to escape.

I gaped at the temple, urging Abram to hurry to me, although I did not know if he knew where I waited. His eyes raked across the crowd in the direction we had run earlier. He found me and I felt a warmth fill me as his eyes met mine. He raced toward me when he reached the ground. The altar complex collapsed behind him, overwhelming the priests who tried to stumble behind him down the stairs and away from the destruction.

Abram caught my hand and we ran far away before stopping. We turned and frowned at the rubble that once was Elkenah's temple. The angel had disappeared, leaving detritus, dust, and devastation.

A few men ran toward the temple. They dragged the broken bodies of the priests away from the danger. The high priest's body convulsed in their arms and stilled. I stared numbly at the destruction.

Abram took my arm. "We must go."

We left the temple complex, emerging into unnaturally quiet streets. Everyone had disappeared into their homes. Abram led me down streets, turning corners, and finally into a narrow alley. He opened a door, rushed through the house, opened a door on the other side, and led me into an alley.

"Whose —" I asked, wanting to hear his voice.

Abram brought a finger to my lips and shook his head. "Later," he mouthed.

I followed him down more streets until relief filled me when at last I saw the home we shared with Abram's father, Terah, and the rest of his family. At the door, we stopped to brush away the dust that had settled on our clothing.

"You bleed," I whispered, touching Abram's forehead softly.

"I will be fine." He pushed the door open and stepped aside while I stepped into the dark coolness of the entry. "We must leave this city. They will blame us for the destruction of the temple."

"We did nothing. You did nothing," I exclaimed. My insides tightened

"Nothing except pray to Jehovah. It will be enough for them to blame us."

Terah limped into the sitting room as we entered. "How did you escape?"

"Jehovah saved me."

How would you know we escaped?

"No one evades the priests of Elkenah."

"How do you know?" Abram asked, echoing my thoughts. "You were in bed sick when we left to observe the sacrifice."

"We would have stayed with you if the law had allowed it," I added. *We would have bruises and sick stomachs if we could have stayed away from the sacrifices.*

Terah fell silent.

I wondered at his knowledge, his silence. *What did he do?*

"Father?" Abram demanded.

"You know I joined the worshipers of Elkenah," Terah whined. His lips trembled. He blinked uncontrollably. "They demand we share any knowledge of those who refuse to worship one of the gods of Ur."

"Jehovah has been a God of Ur since Shem and his sons brought Noah here to live after the languages were confounded at Nimrod's tower. How can they say we who believe Jehovah do not worship a God of Ur?"

"They no longer recognize Jehovah." Beads of sweat covered Terah's forehead.

"Did you give them my name?" Abram asked Terah. His nostrils flared.

My heart pounded as I listened to the men. *Why would Terah turn from Jehovah to Elkenah?*

"No. Not at first. I told them of Onitah's daughters."

"You gave those righteous women up to Elkenah's wicked priests?" Abram's low, tense voice sounded dangerous. "And me?"

"They were not happy with only those three names. They wanted to know who taught them of Jehovah." Terah's voice whined even more than I thought possible. *He has always confidently taken the lead in the family, never showing weakness. What happened to him?*

"And you gave them my name? I, who am your son?" His expression became tight, a vein pumped along his temple.

I sank heavily in the nearest chair. *How could a father do this to his son?* Confusion filled me. I felt exposed.

"They forced me," Terah squeaked. "They threatened to sacrifice me. I had to speak your name." He buried his face in his hands.

I wanted to shout obscenities at the man. How could he give his own son to the priests of Elkenah? It would have been better that they had sacrificed *him*.

Abram echoed my thoughts. "Why? How could you?"

"I trusted Elkenah to save you," Terah whined from behind his quivering hands.

"Elkenah!" Abram exploded. "Elkenah is a god of stone, made by man. Your fathers were all prophets, teaching of Jehovah and warning against false gods. Elkenah did not save me! Only the God of our Fathers could save me!"

Terah dropped his hands enough he could see over his fingers. "How did he do it? Coward that I am, I came home when the priests left the altar looking for you."

"I thought you slept peacefully in your bed," I murmured.

"Only a coward would run and hide, knowing he had sent his son to certain death." Abram shook his head and sat in a chair across from Terah. His lip curled. "Jehovah sent an angel who saved me. In the process, he destroyed the temple of Elkenah and his priests."

Terah gaped at Abram. "They are all dead?"

"All who were in the temple."

"Elkenah did not protect his high priest?" Terah's jaw quivered.

"How could he?" I said. "Elkenah is not a god. He is an idol made of stone by men. He does not live. He is no god. Only Jehovah can save."

"Jehovah told me we must leave," Abram said. "Come Sarai. We must prepare."

Chapter Two

Freedom

I folded the dresses I had pulled from the hooks in my dressing room and set them into the trunks I had brought to my marriage with Abram. I ran my hands over the trunks, remembering the day I brought them into the house.

Abram's parents had been friends with mine. We had been friends throughout my childhood, although he was ten years older than me. I was happy and not a little surprised when Mother advised me about the agreement made between them and Abram's parents. I would become Abram's wife.

In my way, I had loved Abram since my early childhood. He had cared for me and treated me kindly after our marriage. His mother, Ahuva, had welcomed me into her home and treated me fairly. Although I missed Mother, I had been happy in the large home of Terah and Ahuva.

Abram entered our rooms and pulled me into his arms. "Will you be ready to leave soon?"

"I have almost everything prepared. I sent Ela to pack her things. Will we be traveling alone?"

Abram perched on the bed. "Father feels he must go with us. Since he gave the priests my name, he fears for his life."

I shivered. "Do you still trust him? He follows Elkenah." I did not. I folded another dress and set it in the trunk.

"I know. Since Mother died, he has been angry with Jehovah. I do not understand it." He chewed on his beard while I folded three blankets and tucked them into a trunk.

"It looks like Lot and Galya will go with us as well."

"Will Lot leave his parents' graves untended?"

"Lot and Galya still believe in Jehovah. I suppose they should go with us. They will have problems here if they do not." Abram spit out his beard and smoothed it. "Nahor and Milcah are staying here. They will care for Haron's and Chava's graves. Milcah will care for them, or see that they are."

"She would, since she is Lot's sister," I murmured. I still felt the sting of Chava's sly insults as she held her children close. I could not change my childlessness and her jibes only caused me sorrow.

"Do you still love me, Abram?" I asked. I had often questioned his love for me after her taunts, and I reverted to that fear with the memory.

"Love you?" His eyes leapt to my face. "More than ever. Why would you ask?"

"I am barren. I have not given you the children you deserve."

Abram pulled me onto his lap and hugged me. "While the angel caused so much damage at the temple, I heard the voice of Jehovah. He promised me blessings. Among those blessings will be children."

I stiffened. "I am not young."

"You are young enough to have children." Abram said and kissed me.

I leaned back from his kisses. "When?" *How is it possible? I will not speak my concern.*

"I do not know. But it will happen. We must be patient." He crossed his legs and allowed the top leg to swing.

"It will be good to leave the mocking of my sisters." I grabbed another blanket to fold, hiding the tears that fought to trickle down my cheeks.

Abram took my hand and tenderly pulled me into his arms. "Do not allow their mocking to hurt you, Sarai. You are a beautiful woman. I am grateful you agreed to marry me."

"Even when I have not given you children?" I pushed him back and set the corners of the blanket together.

"More every day. You were courageous today." He took the other end of the blanket I held and helped me fold it.

"How was I courageous? I wanted to scream for them to let you go." I shuddered at the memory.

"But you did not. You waited to see how Jehovah would save me."

I tucked the blanket into the trunk. "I did not feel courageous. I felt frightened. What would I do without you?" I could not turn to face him, fearing his response.

"You do not have to know that yet, thank Jehovah." He walked toward the dressing room. "I should gather my clothes."

"Thank Jehovah," I agreed. "No need for that," I called after him.

"Where is my clothing?" Abram asked, stepping back into our sleeping room.

"Ela packed them already. They are with my clothing in that trunk." I pointed with my chin toward the trunk on the floor. "I have most of our possessions packed."

"Did you pack my scrolls? The records of my fathers are important to keep." Until today, I had wondered that Abram's grandfather hand bypassed Terah and given the records to Abram.

"I planned to put them on top of this trunk," I said, nodding toward the shelf where he kept the scrolls. I did not want them folded or bent."

He walked to the shelf and pulled one scroll off. "Adam's Book of Commandments. I am blessed to have a copy of this. Few men received a copy."

"Your father is sad you received a copy when he did not."

"Father forgot to obey Jehovah's laws," Abram said in a flat voice.

"Yes, but he does not like to be told that."

"He offered me up for sacrifice!" Heat rose in his voice.

I set a hand on his arm. "And Jehovah will punish him for that heinous crime."

Abram took a deep breath and let it out slowly. "I do not know if I can travel with him."

"There will be others with us. Lot and Galya will bring servants. So will Terah." I pulled more scrolls from the shelf and set them in the top of the trunk.

"Yitzhak is coming with us as well. He insists we will need his help caring for the animals."

"He is probably correct. We will need many animals to carry us and our possessions."

Abram ticked the numbers on his fingers. "Camels for each of us, five of us in our family, five or more servants, and animals to carry our trunks. Yes, there will be many animals. We will need Yitzhak."

I put the last of Abram's book scrolls in the trunk.

"There. We are ready to leave."

"Almost," Abram said. He rolled the bed we slept on and, with my help, tied it in three places. "Now we are ready."

I opened the door to our rooms and found servants ready to carry our trunks and bed down the stairs. I stepped aside and allowed them to work. I scanned the space Abram and I had shared for so many years. *Will I ever see this room again? Will I miss it? Perhaps, but I do not want to fear the priests' retribution. Better to leave.*

When the servants had gathered everything and marched down the stairs, Abram took my hand. "It is time. We must leave."

The sun dipped close to the mountains as our small company approached Ur's western gate. My heart pounded when I saw guards standing in the way of our freedom. After the destruction of the largest temple in the city, would they allow our family to leave?

Abram kicked his camel to move a little faster and met the guard ahead of the rest of us. He spoke to them and they laughed together before the guards lifted their swords in salute to them. Abram waved the others forward. People, camels, donkeys, and herds of sheep and goats kicked up dust as we passed the gates and the guards. He rode beside me through the gate and into the setting sun.

I had seen sunsets from within the city of Ur, but outside the walls, the golden sky glowed in front of us in a way different than I had ever experienced. I moved forward on my camel with the others while I gazed into the colors of the setting sun. Purples, violets, pinks, and oranges joined the golden glow.

"Sarai?" Abram asked.

I dragged my eyes from the beauty of the sunset and turned to him. "Yes?"

"Jehovah painted the sky beautiful colors to welcome us into the wilderness."

"Beautiful," I breathed. "I have never seen so many colors in a setting sun."

Terah rode forward to move beside Abram. "There are clouds in the distance. The storm out there is what colors the sky."

I squinted into the distance, only now seeing the clouds. "Will we be safe?"

"Jehovah will protect us," Abram said, and squinted at Terah, who had fallen back, and shook his head. "He would not bring us into the wilderness to destroy us. If He wanted that, He would have allowed the priests to sacrifice me."

Our small company rode into the dusk, allowing our animals to pick their way through the wilderness, their path lit by the moon shining round, full, and bright.

After traveling for what seemed like hours, Abram called us to a halt. "I hear the trickling of water. We will camp here tonight and move on tomorrow." I expected to hear more fatigue in his voice, but he hid it from the others.

"Where are we going?" Lot asked. "Do you know our destination?"

"For tonight, here. Tomorrow, I do not know. Jehovah leads us."

I slid off my camel and stretched with a groan. I had never ridden that long. Where would I go in Ur? Even with my cushioned seat, exhaustion filled me. I moaned at the thought of sitting atop the animal the next day.

The men joined manservants and soon had a small fire burning, tents set up, and the animals settled. I helped the women cook a small meal, retrieving food from baskets.

Yawning and stretching, Abram and I entered our tent after we ate. We said our nightly prayers and lay on our bed. I slept with Abram's hand in mine.

I had not dozed long when he shook me awake. *Is it morning already? Has the night passed?* It seemed too soon. But no darkness shrouded the tent. I could see no light through the space near the door. "Is —" I whispered.

"Listen," he whispered, covering my mouth.

Men's rough, whispering voices grumbled outside the tent.

"This has to be them," one whispered.

"How do we know this is the one?" another asked.

"The guards pointed the way. They only allowed one group of people to leave Ur this evening. They said the man joked with them about the fall of the temple. Who would do that?"

I sucked in my breath behind Abram's hand and stared wildly inside the tent. His other hand found mine and squeezed it.

Why did the guards allow us to leave, only to send men out to attack us? Was this their plan all along?

"Jehovah sent us here. He will protect us." Abram's whispered words tickled my ear.

"The priests of Libnah want these people for the next sacrifice," a man whispered from the dark outside.

"If we take them back. I say we kill them here," another replied.

"You know what Libnah's priests will do if we do not take them back."

"They said he would mark the tent of the escaped one."

"He? Which he?" I murmured. My hands were slippery with sweat.

Abram shook his head.

"He did not mark a tent."

"Where are they?" the frustrated voice of a man growled.

"I cannot see in the dark."

"We need a fire. Get a firebrand."

I nodded and pulled Abram's hand from my mouth. I sucked in a soft breath and looked to him for directions.

A flash of a fire brand lit the air outside our tent.

We sat on our bed, making no noise, for many long minutes while the men searched through the camp. Their shadows danced through the tent. I swallowed the knot in my throat. *Jehovah, protect us!*

"I see the tents, but I cannot get close to them."

"Press harder. The priests demand these people for sacrifice."

Why are they not entering our tents?

"I cannot push through. The space is like stone."

"We will burn them out," a man cried.

The fire brand wavered, then moved away toward Terah's tent.

I glanced at Abram. "What should we do?" I mouthed.

"Wait," he mouthed back.

Terah shouted as he tumbled from his tent. The fire brand bounced on the ground but did not go out. It must have landed close to his tent, for another light began to blaze close to the ground.

Abram moved to his knees and prayed softly to Jehovah. As he prayed, thunder echoed across the valley. The heavens opened and rain fell in a deluge. No gentle pitter-patter on the roof announced its arrival. Instead, it pounded on the tent and everywhere else.

We were saved! Jehovah had blessed us.

Lightning struck near our tent, lighting the space. Shadows of the men bounced momentarily off our tent. A man outside screamed. The others shouted. More lightning struck. Their shadows scattered. I barely heard their horses' hooves splatter through the mud and water.

Abram's voice lifted in a prayer of thanksgiving. I joined him.

"What happened?" I asked after the amen.

"Someone betrayed us," Abram said. "But Jehovah protected us once more."

"What about Terah? Did his tent burn?"

Abram peeked through the tent door, then pulled his head back. "Father's tent did not burn. He must have returned inside when the rain began, for I do not see him now."

"Did you see any damage?"

"It is too dark and rainy to see anything. We will find out in the morning."

Abram lay back down and pulled me close to him. "We are blessed. All will be well."

I snuggled close to him, and listened to him breathe. Abram had promised Jehovah's protection. I sighed, grateful He had done as promised once more.

Chapter Three

Escape

When I slipped out of the tent to prepare for the day, I stared in disbelief at the devastation. Trees had blown over in the wind and rain. Water ran through our camp. The little stream we heard trickling the night before had swollen into a flooding river.

Yet, as I absorbed the surrounding destruction, none of our tents had blown over. The camels lay with their backs to the wind. Donkeys, sheep, and goats lay near them, all patiently waiting for the men to feed them. Even the food left beside the fire pit had not moved, nor had the pounding rain drenched it.

"Thank you, Jehovah," I said, glancing upward.

Abram stepped through the tent door and took in the destruction surrounding us as I had. "Jehovah is good. He blessed us once one more."

"What happened last night?" Galya asked. "I dreamed of men outside our tents, searching for us, wanting to bind us and return us to Ur as sacrifices to Libnah. Then I dreamed it rained and drove them away."

"I dreamed the same," Lot said. "It is strange we would have the same dream."

"You did not dream," Abram said. "Men came into our camp last night, desperately seeking to return us as sacrifices to Libnah."

Terah exited his tent, rubbing his eyes. "You did not hear me shout?"

"Did you shout?" Galya asked.

"They tried to burn Father's tent," Abram said.

Lot scowled, searching for evidence of the men. "But the animals are here. They did not scatter or take them."

I glanced at the camels and donkeys. "And they are hungry. How did it happen? They are still here?"

As I spoke, men servants stepped from their tent.

"We were careful to tie them so no one could free them easily last night," Yitzhak said. "We feared the priests of the temples would send someone to attack us."

"You were more aware than we were," Abram said. "I did not think of that, although I should have. We are blessed to have your awareness. Thank you, Yitzhak."

I took Abram's hand. "You had other things to consider."

"But I should have considered the possibility the priests would send their thugs to attack us. The rain blessed us."

Before I could comment further, Abram left my side, helping the servants to care for the animals. Lot and Terah followed him.

"I suppose it is up to us to begin our morning meal," Galya said.

I nodded and joined Galya and rummaged through the trunk for food to prepare. Ela rushed from her tent, followed by Nitza, Galya's servant.

"My ladies! We are here to help with those things," Ela exclaimed.

"But my mother taught —" I said.

"And she taught you well, but you have me to cook," Ela said.

"I did not know you cooked."

My mother cooks for Terah's house, or she did when Terah lived there. Now she cooks for Nahor and Milcah and their family. Someone needs to help them."

Galya and I nodded at the same time. Milcah would need help, especially since we had both left the house.

"Milcah must be loving the freedom as mistress of the house," Galya said, waggling her eyebrows.

"I hope she has learned enough from us and her mother," I said, pursing my lips.

"If not," Nitza said, smiling at us, "our mother will be there to guide and help her until she has. Do not fear. Mother will help her."

"We both learned to cook from her at a young age. Mother did not want us to be unprepared for our service to others," Ela added, gathering up the needed supplies for the morning meal.

"And she will help Milcah," Nitza said, bending to stir the fire.

I allowed the tension that built up in the memory of Milcah to release. I had not had time to worry about her in the rush to leave Ur and with the bandits during the night. "Good. That gives me one less thing to worry about."

Galya laughed. "As though you will stop worrying about Milcah. As long as I have known you, you care about others and show your concern with worry."

"That is something I must repent of," I said with a smile.

"Caring for others?" Galya asked, her eyebrows dipping low over her eyes.

I giggled. "No, silly. Worrying so much about others that it shows."

Nitza and Ela nudged Galya and me away from the food trunks. "We will prepare the morning food. You go prepare yourselves to look beautiful for the ride ahead. The men will want to leave soon after we eat."

Galya and I turned to stroll back to our tents. "You should allow others to make their mistakes," she said.

"I know. How else can we learn? But ..."

"You do not need to mother me or the servants. We can make our own mistakes."

Galya tucked her arm through mine and walked with me to our tents.

Do I mother the other women? Perhaps because I miss mothering a child of my own. I know others need to learn, and they do, but I want to be certain they do.

"Now, go get ready for the day," Galya said, nudging me toward my tent.

I set my fists on my hips. "Who is giving orders now?"

Innocence filled her eyes. "Not me. I merely gave you a suggestion. You can take it or not. However, if you do not, it will be you who will cause our men's frustration."

I tipped my head back and laughed. "Right you are. I will be ready for the day before you."

"A race?" Galya asked.

"Why not?"

I stepped through my tent door and opened the trunk with my clothing in it. Abram had set it beside the tent wall the night before. I lifted out the clothing I wanted to wear that day and set it on the bed, then stripped off my sleeping clothing. I poured water into a bowl for washing, then dipped a cloth into the water.

Gritting my teeth at the cold of the cloth, I quickly washed my body and pulled the clean clothing over my head. I tucked my dirty clothing into a basket, then set it in the clothing trunk, knowing it could be some time before we had time and water to wash clothing.

As I looked at the tent, considering what else needed to be done, Abram entered. "Good," he said. "You are ready. I will roll up the bed so Yitzhak can take down the tent."

"Do you need my help?" I asked.

"No. Go help Ela and Nitza with the meal. We will get our baggage loaded."

I stepped from my tent as Galya stepped from hers, fully dressed and ready to go. "Are you ready for the day?"

"I am. It looks like we were both fast," she said with a grin.

"It has been a long time since I saw you dress and prepare for the day so fast," I teased.

Galya harrumphed and lifted her chin. "I can be fast if I want. I rarely want that."

"That will change."

She frowned. "Why would it change?"

"We will have to be ready to travel when the men are ready."

"They can wait," Galya grumbled.

"Can they?"

The rocking gait of riding on my camel made me feel drowsy, especially after the excitement of men attempting to attack us the night before. Sun beat down on us, making me even more sleepy.

"I wonder who those men spoke of last night," Abram murmured.

"Who?" I murmured through sleep-hazed eyes.

"When they said 'he' would mark the tent for them. Who would mark our tent? Who would know which tent was ours?"

Instantly wide awake, my head jerked toward him. *Who would mark our tent? One of ours? Surely not.* "Someone marked our tent? Why would they do that?"

"I do not know who would do that. While we prepared and packed each tent this morning, I watched for a mark. I found a black spot on the back of our tent. Someone had marked it. Who among our company would do that for the priests? How would they know we would leave?"

"We escaped from the temple. It would be reasonable for us to want to leave Ur. The priests of Elkenah —"

My camel swayed as it stepped past a bush in its path. I lurched to the side, then regained my seat, before I guided it back to walk near Abram.

"And the priests of the other gods. Libnah ordered these men to come for us," Abram reminded me.

"They would all be angry with us. If we stayed and other priests tried to take and sacrifice you ..." my voice drifted off. The possibilities took my breath away.

Abram's camel spit into the wind. Some splattered back onto me. I frowned and thought about cursing it. Instead, I pulled my cloth from my bag, worn across my shoulder and wiped the spittle from my face, then pulled my head covering over my face.

"Would Jehovah send another angel to save me?" Abram sucked in his breath. "I do not want to try Him. He told me to leave. Because I did, He will protect us as He did last night."

I considered his words before speaking again. I tried to keep worry from edging my voice. "But there is still the same problem."

"What is that?"

"Who marked our tent? It would have to be someone in our family or one of our servants."

"Yes. And," Abram's voice dropped so the others could not hear him over the noise of the animals. He looked about us to see if others were near before he spoke. "Is the traitor still in Ur or did he come with us?"

"Come with us?" my voice neared a squeal.

Abram lifted a finger to his lips. "We do not want him to know we know there is a traitor among us."

"*If* he came with us," I added. "He could have been a servant who stayed behind to help Nahor and Milcah."

Abram nodded. "How can we discover him if he is here?"

His camel took him on the other side of a tree before he guided it to trundle beside mine.

"Who did not exclaim about the noise of men outside?" I asked.

"None. All the men servants chattered excitedly about the interruption to their sleep while we fed and cared for the animals."

"He may know we would look for him," I said.

"Would it be a servant?"

"Who else would it be?" My gaze flicked from the distant haze to Abram's eyes.

"Father gave me up to the priests of Elkenah. Would he have also marked our tent?"

My eyes widened. *He has changed much in the years since Ahuva's death. Would he still desire to bow to the priests of Elkenah?* "Terah seemed contrite yesterday."

"Yes, and the priests convinced him to name me." Bitterness filled Abram's voice and pinched his face.

"You do not trust your own father?" I peered toward the horizon as my camel swayed around a big rock. This time I had prepared, and moved with it. When I looked at Abram again, his eyes were closed.

When he opened his eyes, he shook his head. "I do not know what my father will do. I thought I did, but he has changed. The priests of Elkenah changed his heart, or he did. He is repentant now, but how long will it last? Elkenah has a powerful pull for weak men."

"Your father is not weak!" *Something has changed. I heard and saw it yesterday. I never thought of him as weak before. I could not now.*

"He was not weak before Mother died. He stayed strong for her. Her love for Jehovah and him helped him stay strong. But since she died ..." Abram sucked in a deep breath and swallowed. "Since she returned to Jehovah, Father blames Him for her death. I saw him go looking for another god to worship."

I sighed. "I noticed that too. I hoped it was only me seeing things."

"I hoped the same thing, but after yesterday ... after he admitted giving my name and the names of Onofria, Hathor, and Ain to the priests, I see it more clearly. He has changed."

"But would he mark our tent for the thugs the priests sent?"

Abram shrugged. "I do not know."

I juggled the reins in my hands. "If not him, who?"

Abram glowered into the distance, then let his eyes trace the land. "I do not know."

We rode in silence for almost an hour. I peeked at him occasionally, but his eyes glazed over, deep in thought.

Who would hate us enough to mark us for the priests? Who would know the priests would follow and try to capture us, or at least Abram?

My thoughts spun in circles, considering one, then another of the members of our household in Ur. It could not have been them. Or could it? Who outside our home would know we were leaving and had access to mark the tent?

Too many questions.

I stared at the surrounding land. I had not left Ur before. My parents, and after them, Abram, kept me close to home for protection. Besides, where would I go outside the gates? Ur held everything I needed. Shops. Other women to gossip with. Jehovah. What more did I need?

However, here I was, away from the protective walls of Ur. The land was beautiful. We passed through lush green meadows surrounded by tall green trees and sprinkled with colorful flowers. The priests had gardens, but nothing like this.

Priests. Bah. Why allow them to enter my thoughts? Those priests were cruel, hateful men. Their gods were greedy, violent, and bloody. Not like the one true God, Jehovah. He loved his people and wanted them to return to him.

Elkenah had come from Egypt. I had heard that in the beginning, Pharoah had believed in Jehovah, but something happened over the years. Somehow the worship had changed to false gods. Bloody gods who demanded the sacrifice of children and virgins.

I shivered. How could a woman give up her child to be sacrificed? My empty arms ached for a child. I would never give up one of my children as a sacrifice.

I shook my head and glanced once more at Abram, riding in silence beside me with an unblinking stare at the land.

"We should stop soon for our midday meal while there are still trees for shade and a stream to refill our water. The land will change soon." His voice broke the silence.

I flinched and looked up to see the sun near its apex. "Yes. It is near midday."

"Do you have food that is easy to eat? We will not want to stop for long, lest priests send their men to attack us again."

At my nod, Abram raised his fist for the others to see and slowed. He moved closer to the trees and stopped. The rest of us followed him, glad of the opportunity to rest. My back and legs ached and my eyes burned. I welcomed a brief rest off the back of the camel.

Abram signaled to my animal to kneel and helped me off.

"The women are not accustomed to riding on camels," Lot said as he slid off his.

"No. It will be difficult for them to ride all day, but they must. We must get far away from the priests and their men," Abram said.

"Do you think they will return after last night?" Lot asked.

"Anything is possible. We must be watchful."

"We probably should have taken a ship up the Euphrates to Harran," Abram told me later that day as we traveled through a mountain pass.

"Or let the city guards think we would," I suggested. "That is a long way to Canaan."

"Probably no longer than it will take us to travel on these camels. It is too late to change our path now. I suspect we will be safer this way. Jehovah did not tell me to escape by racing up the Euphrates. He told me to escape across the land. We may not go all the way to Canaan."

"Then He will protect us as He did last night. Jehovah would not send us away from Ur merely to have the priests' men capture us," I said.

Wind blew down the mountain into our faces. I tugged my robe closer to me and pulled my headscarf over my face. Abram had shown the women how to pull our scarves across our faces to protect us from the wind and dust.

Nitza had scoffed at the thought of needing to protect her face. "We ride through a beautiful meadow and trees. No dust will blow into our eyes."

"You will see, Nitza," Abram had said.

Now, Nitza cried and rubbed at the dust in her face as the wind blew bits of dust and broken plants into her eyes.

I turned back to frown at her. "She should have listened. I will go help her."

"Do not be gone long. I do not want you far from me. I do not trust the priests' men."

"I will hurry back," I said and turned to ride back along the line of camels and people. Nitza rode near the back with the animals carrying tents and trunks, close to the sheep and goats. "Why are you so far to the back, Nitza?"

"Am I? I cannot see."

I leaned close to her. "Let me help." With quick, practiced hands, I arranged Nitza's scarf to protect her face.

She sighed when she could see again without having to fight her scarf, the wind, and all the dust. "How did I get so far to the back?" She frowned at the animals that trotted beside her.

"You did not listen when Abram gave instructions. Listen next time."

Nitza nodded with a frown and kicked her camel to make it move faster. I turned and urged my ride forward at a lope. Nitza reached Ela and the other servants and slowed to ride with them. I passed them and rode on toward the front to ride beside Abram.

He lifted his arm and spun it in a circle. Those who were behind him bunched up near him.

"The wind is too strong. We need to find cover. Did anyone see a cave or anywhere we could hide from this wind?"

The men turned, looking at the hills. None seemed available.

"I see a big log fall," Terah said, pointing.

I squinted in the direction Terah pointed. I could scarcely see the log fall through the dirt in the wind. I followed Abram toward it, bent over my camel's back, trying to hide from the wind and dirt. The others followed us.

As we neared the fall, the wind dropped. The log fall protected us from the wind. We crowded as close to the logs as we could, bringing the animals close to protect them from blowing dirt and other debris.

We huddled together near the logs, for the wind blew away our words. I snuggled close to Abram. *When will this wind stop? I fear the priests' men will find us again.*

I must have dozed. I dreamed of men blowing past on the trail, pushed by the wind. They struggled to stay mounted on their horses, and finally dismounted, using them as a shield. Some lost their way and were separated from the others. Soon, they all slumped to the ground, overcome by the storm.

Abram nudged me in the ribs. "We can go now. The storm has passed."

I looked up in confusion. Where had the wind gone? "I dreamed —"

Abram set a finger to my lips. "It was no dream."

I shuddered. *Sad that men would lose their way like that. All are precious to Jehovah.* I refused to allow tears to betray me.

We shook the dirt from our clothing, preparing to leave. After drinking from our water jugs, and watering the animals, we climbed on our camels and returned to the trail.

"We are safe from the priests' men now," Abram said.

"How do you know?" Terah asked.

"The wind has swept away all evidence of our passing. If any continue to follow us, they will not find us when our trail is gone."

I allowed the fear within me to escape in a sigh. We could travel without fear. The priests could not force us to return to Ur and sacrifice.

As we rode on, strange lumps of dirt appeared along the side of the trail. Some seemed to resemble stretched out arms or legs. Larger lumps had the appearance of a horse. We passed several of these. I repressed the horror I felt with a shudder. It was not a dream.

"That one looks like a man curled up to get out of the wind," Ela said.

"Look, an arm reaching for help," Nitza said.

"That looks like a horse," Galya said, laughter filling her voice.

I shuddered. She did not see what I saw during the windstorm, or she would not laugh now.

"It could be," Lot said in a hushed voice. "Perhaps men followed us."

After that, we rode past the strange lumps of dirt and sand in awed silence. Grief and horror flitting across the faces of the company. Were these the men who followed us? Men who succumbed to the storm? How sad for them. Worse for their families. During the rest of the day, I thought about these men, wondering if they had wives and children. Perhaps they were so cruel they did not? I shook my head and wiped a tear from my cheek.

Abram and I rode in the front again. He leaned close and took my hand. "They do not deserve your tears," he murmured.

"But their mothers do."

Chapter Four

Rose and Thorn

Days later, our tired and dirty caravan entered the gates of Harran. No one would confuse our little village with this great city with one look at their gates. Harran's simple gates, made of tall wooden posts, did not glint in the sun as the copper gates of Ur. Harran had fewer homes and shops, and their temples were small. Perhaps their priests would have less power than those of Ur.

"Have you been here before?" I asked Abram.

He nodded his head. "Yes. I came to trade a few years ago. I brought samples of our best wool. Only Meir showed an interest at first. The others did not, and they had little to trade with me. Meir worked with our wool, dying and spinning it into beautiful fabrics. I will find his shop tomorrow. He will help us locate a place to live." Abram shook his head. "Since my last visit, Harran has grown."

"Grown?" My eyes widened. "How small was it?"

"A little hamlet. I wondered why Jehovah would send us here. How can we hide in such a small village? But Jehovah knows. Harran has grown big enough to absorb a family of our size without comment." He searched along the streets.

"Where will we stay?"

"I am looking for an inn. We must travel closer to the city center to find a safe one."

"You want to go to the city center with all these animals?" I asked, looking back at our caravan.

"Perhaps not to the center, but to a better location than near the wall. That is where the thieves congregate, hoping to take what is not theirs."

I kept my comments about the size of this "city" to myself as I followed Abram along the twisting streets into the city. It amazed me he could find his way in a city, no matter that it was much smaller than Ur, without getting lost. I could not have done that.

Tall, rounded roofs, looking much like beehives, poked above the buildings. I wondered why they looked like that. How did they figure out how to build roofs like that?

Our camels' feet clacked on the streets paved with rocks. Donkeys, sheep, and goats noisily expressed their distaste of the cramped streets. Their commotion, louder than it was in the wilderness, made me flinch. I feared we would draw the attention of priests who would try to send us back to Ur. As we passed closer to the center of the city, the populace covered the sound of our animals.

People surrounded us, hardly noticing our passing. Those who did glowered up at the lanky camels and back at all the animals that trailed behind. I wondered if we should dismount, but when I looked at Abram, he shook his head and continued riding.

The smell of our animals was pleasant compared to the stench of garbage and filth flowing down the center of the dirty streets. I pulled my scarf over my face to hide from the aroma. Ur would have fined these people. But Ur would have also killed my Abram and would possibly have tried to sacrifice me. I would cheerfully trade the filth in these streets for the certain death in Ur.

The crowd swarmed around us. "Will our animals get lost?" I asked Abram.

"No. The camels are tall enough to be seen by those who herd the other animals. They will not lose them."

Another noisy caravan passed us with men only riding camels and trailing no other animals. They traveled away from the center of the city. Abram stopped the leader to ask about a safe place to bed down our animals.

"The Camel's Ear is a safe inn, and they have room for many animals. Others stay there now, but there is room for your caravan."

"Where is the Camel's Ear?" Abram asked.

"On down this road, turn left at the third street, then it is on your right."

Abram nodded and thanked the man. After the other caravan passed us, he turned right.

"I thought he said left and on down the street," I said.

"He did, but I have heard of that inn. It is not safe to stay there with women. We will go to the Rose and Thorn. I have stayed there before."

"Will it not be as dangerous?"

Abram took my hand. "If it is, we will find another place to stay. I have friends who live there. Good friends whom I trust."

I tugged my scarf across my face once more to shield me from the reek and followed him. His camel marched through twisting streets until I was certain Abram had forgotten where to find this inn. When he stopped, the street held fewer people.

"We are here," he said.

I gazed at the building, wondering where 'here' was. He pointed at a signboard hanging on a chain over his head. A red rose with a green thorn peeping from beneath the rose announced the inn.

"The Rose and Thorn," he announced.

"This is not near the center of town," Lot said, riding up to stand beside Abram. "Are you certain it will be safe?"

"I have stayed here before. The owner, Tal, is my friend."

"If your friend still owns the place," Terah said, pushing up next to Abram.

"I will go see," Abram said, signaling to his camel to settle to the ground.

Lot followed. "I will go with you. It is not safe to go inside these inns alone."

Abram grumbled softly about his ability to meet an old friend alone, then nodded. "Father, please stay out here with the women and our baggage. Someone must protect them."

Terah complained under his breath that he should be the one ensuring their safety. But he sat straight, watching everywhere while we waited for Abram and Lot to return.

Tall buildings made of bricks surrounded us. Bricks. They built buildings in Ur of stone. Were these people so poor? But they have those interesting roofs. Strange.

Doors opened into the buildings off the main road. I gawked at them, trying to discover what was in each. A tavern? Perhaps, but most inns included taverns. Homes? Workshops? Perhaps shops? The town was so different from Ur, I hoped to find familiar things.

After waiting for what seemed a long time, a gate in the wall near the Rose and Thorn opened and Abram and a short, portly man exited. Abram waved to our herders, inviting them to bring the sheep and goats inside. He walked over to those of us who waited for him with the man from the inn.

"This is Tal, owner of the Rose and Thorn," Abram said, introducing his friend after helping me dismount. "Tal, may I introduce you to my wife, Sarai, my father, Terah, my nephew, Lot, you know, and his wife, Galya?"

"I am humbled to meet you," Tal said. "Your Abram is a wonderful friend and an honest trader."

I had no doubts about his kindness and honesty. I hoped this Tal would treat us the same.

After we greeted him, Tal invited us inside his inn. As we entered, I peered at the dim room, lit only by candles. Tables were scattered throughout the small space. Men sipped at the ale in front of them. A wide bar was set along one side of the room. Behind it stood a short, squat woman dressed in a simple dress, covered by a bright apron, spotted with ale and food. Above the apron, a huge grin on a cheerful face welcomed me.

"I am Nita, that big man's wife."

"Big?" I asked. Big of stomach, perhaps.

"Big of stature and big-hearted, I am the rose and he is the thorn," she said, tipping her head back in laughter.

I gaped at Tal, who quietly chuckled.

"Tal is a good man," Nita said. "He helps too many people, which sometimes causes us trouble." She winked at my Abram. "But your man never was one to bring us grief."

Abram set his hand against his heart and bent at the waist slightly. "I thank you for the kind words. I pray I can continue in your high esteem."

My eyes widened at their banter.

"You must be hungry," Nita said.

"Hungry and in need of a bath," I answered. "We have traveled many days. A hot bath would be lovely."

"We can help with that. Sit. I will feed you first, then you can bathe and rest." Nita directed us to one of the empty tables. "I will have food here for you soon."

She disappeared behind a door. Delicious fragrances slipped past, causing my stomach to gurgle. I set my hand on it and urged it to still.

Soon Nita led a parade of women carrying dishes, each dish covered with a cloth. They set these in front of us. When the women removed the cloths, they had placed warm bread and a hot cabbage and mutton soup in front of us. It smelled heavenly. We had eaten that morning, so I should not have been hungry. But the fragrance of the food stirred my stomach's noises.

After a quiet prayer, Abram lifted his spoon and dipped it into the soup. "Delicious!" he announced.

I ate, dipping warm, yeasty bread, slavered with butter, into the soup as well as spooning the chunks of vegetables and mutton from the bowl. Sooner than I wanted, the bowl was empty.

"More?" Nita asked.

I pushed back from the table. "It was wonderful, but the hot bath calls to me. Can you show us to our rooms?"

"Your servants carried your luggage up while you ate." She saw me squint. "Do not fear. We will feed your servants, too." *How did she know I worried about my servants?*

Nita led us up a stone staircase that turned twice on the way up. I nodded. Wise to have that bend. We could observe strangers in the main room without them seeing us.

She led us down a long hall toward the back. "It is quieter back here. You will not hear the noise from the street."

I blinked up into the high roof. Would birds or bats live up there?

After opening our door and handing Abram the key, she stepped aside to show us a tub filled with steaming hot water.

Almost an hour later, I emerged from the tub, only because the water had cooled. Abram laughed as he wrapped the long drying cloth around my body. "You are covered with wrinkles."

"It was worth it to rest in that hot water. It washed away the cares of travel along with the dirt. I think I will survive now."

"Rest," Abram said, helping me into a soft sleeping robe. "We will have a long evening."

I lifted my eyebrows. "Oh?"

"I sent a message to Meir. He invited us to dinner at his home. Tal will be sad, but we need to discuss business."

"Will he help us find a home?" I asked, laying on the bed our servants had unrolled for us.

"I hope he will. I plan to ask him. We need a home. I do not want to live in an inn, even one as nice as this."

His eyes bounced from one side to the other of our room. The shutters covering the window blocked out most of the light, smell, and sounds of the animals and city below us. Candles had been let to light the room before we entered. One wall was covered with a smoke-covered, yet beautiful tapestry depicting deer in a forest. Another wall held a fireplace, laid and ready to be lit. I glanced up at the ceiling. No rounding upward. It had been cut into the tall roof space.

I lay on the bed and Abram pulled the blanket over me, kissing me tenderly. "What will you do while I rest?"

"I must see to the animals and talk with Tal. He will give me some guidance on finding a good place to live. Do not fear, I will set Yitzhak to guard our door. You will be safe."

He blew out all but one candle before pulling the door closed behind him. I closed my eyes, thinking about a new home, one that would be mine finally, not Abram's mother. I could decorate it the way I wanted, do the things I chose. I sighed and slept.

I woke with a start and jumped out of bed. I stood in the middle of the dark room, dressed only in my sleeping robe, wondering what had caused me to waken. Then I heard a soft thud against the door, as if someone had fallen against it.

Fear clogged my throat. Had some enemy overwhelmed Yitzhak? Had he fallen?

I leaned close to the door and listened to a scuffle on the other side. Thumps and bumps were interspersed with groans. Had someone tried to secretly overwhelm my guard?

I knelt near the door and begged Jehovah to protect Yitzhak and me from whomever was attacking us. Panic sent fear tingling along my spine.

A shout echoed in the hallway, and yells joined the bumps and thumps. I continued to pray for our safety and that Yitzhak would not lose the skirmish.

Eventually, the bumping ended. I moved next to the door and leaned on it, unwilling for it to open. Enemy priests may have found us.

The door shifted, bumping against my body. *Who?*

"Sarai? Open the door," Abram said.

I gasped and moved far enough away he could open it. I fell into his arm with a sob. "I heard the sounds of a fight and feared a priest had come for us. I prayed for Yitzhak."

Abram held me close and smoothed my hair. "It is good you prayed for him. It was a priest, or one of his men. I do not know how he found us, but he will not return to his master."

I pulled back from Abram's warm embrace. "What did you do? Is he …?" I stammered.

"No. I did not kill him, but he will not return to Ur. I sent him to be judged by the local law. They will not allow him to leave."

Judged? Would he ever escape and attack us? Would they condemn him to death? My eyes rounded as I stared at my good husband. "Is that better?"

"It is for him. He still lives. We insisted they sell him to a city far from here, and not in Ur. He will not bother us again."

"Will the priests send another man?" A shiver ran through my body.

Abram pulled me close once more. If I could spend more of my time here, I would always feel safe. "I do not know. I only know you are safe and that is what matters to me. I would be sad if he had captured you and taken you back to Ur."

"I would be more than sad. I would be angry."

Abram shook his head and nuzzled my hair. "Jehovah is a loving God. He will not allow you to be taken, nor allow me to be sacrificed. We have blessings waiting for us."

"How can that be? I have never conceived."

"It will happen. Trust Jehovah."

I sighed and snuggled into his embrace. In his arms, I could believe anything, even that I would have children and be a mother of many.

Someone at the door cleared their throat softly. I stepped away, but Abram held my hand. Ela stood in our doorway.

"Nita sent me to tell you your driver is here. I came to see if you need my help to dress," she said.

"A driver?"

"Meir said he would send a driver for us. We are going there for dinner," Abram said. "I did not have time to tell you."

I smiled and brushed at my sleeping robe. "I could use some help, please."

"I will go let our driver know. Do not be long," Abram said, pointing a finger at Ela and me.

I pouted, then laughed at his finger pointing in my direction. "I will not be long."

Less than half an hour later, I descended the stairs, dressed in a clean caftan with my hair piled up on top of my head. Abram ogled up the stairs at me and grinned. His grins always warmed my heart. He met me at the bottom and pulled me close.

"Be wary of what you say while this man can hear," he whispered into my ear. "I do not trust him to keep our location a secret."

I nodded. "I will stay silent. Will that work?"

"Wonderfully." Abram led me toward the man waiting at a table. "Kadir, may I present my wife, Sarai? She is worth the wait."

My face reddened at his words, but rather than saying anything, I smiled and nodded to the man.

"Meir is waiting," Kadir said in a rough voice. "We should go."

He led the way out of the serving room. I waved to Nita as I followed. Her frown frightened me. She did not like this man any more than Abram. My hands slid along my belt where my knife hung, hidden in the folds of my dress. This Kadir would not find me helpless.

Abram opened the door of a small, dirty, nondescript carriage. Mud from a long ago rain still caked the outside. I expected it to smell. I grimaced as Abram helped me inside. I expected a rough ride. Inside, however, soft cushions on comfortable seats greeted me. Abram tied his horse to the back of the carriage before joining me inside.

"Kadir must have brought his best carriage for us," Abram said with a low whistle.

"Or Meir has learned not to show his wealth to others." I leaned back in my seat. "How far is it to Meir's?"

"Kadir said it is not far, but far enough we would want a ride."

"I enjoy riding in a carriage after our journey on the camels. Why did you bring your horse along?"

"I do not know for certain. It seemed to be the right thing to do." Abram took my hand as he seated himself next to me.

During the ride, he shared some tidbits of information about Harran. "This city began as a merchant outpost along a trade route," he said. "We are on the edge of the plains of the Tigris River."

"I would expect the river to help cool the valley," I said, waving my fan in front of my face.

"You would think so, but we are near the desert. The moisture of the river is too far away to cool the city."

Soon, the carriage stopped, and Abram opened the door. He helped me step from the carriage into a small courtyard of a strange looking home.

Kadir nodded toward the front of the house, much like the others of this small city, with tall, rounded roofs, where a couple waited.

The man and woman strode toward us. "Thank you, Kadir, for bringing my friend here," the man said, handing him a small bag of coins.

Kadir bowed slightly to him before untying Abram's horse. Abram took the reins and led the horse to the front of the house and tied him. He gave him a bag of oats to eat while he waited for us.

Kadir and his carriage rattled out of the small courtyard, leaving a sudden silence.

"I am Meir," the tall, dark-haired man said, extending his hand to take mine. He clasped my hand briefly before letting it go. I had no fear of being with him.

Abram joined us and clasped upper arms with Meir. "So good to see you again. This is my beautiful wife, Sarai."

Meir turned to the woman beside him. "And this lovely lady is my wife, Nuriye." Nuriye had lovely, wavy, dark auburn hair and blue eyes.

Nuriye stepped forward and kissed my cheek. "You are welcome to our home, Sarai. We have looked forward to seeing our friend once more. It has been much too long."

She brushed her lips across Abram's cheek.

"Come. Dinner is waiting for us."

Chapter Five

Harran

As we shared our life stories during Nuriye's delicious meal, we became close friends. Her bright blue eyes danced as she laughed and shared. She wept as we shared the story of our escape from Ur. She and Meir were amazed as Abram told of the men who came to take us back to Ur, the storm that drove them home, and the sandstorm that overwhelmed them.

"You two are truly blessed," Meir said, bending his head in a low bow to us. "Your Jehovah surely protects you."

"It is true, He does," Abram said.

Later, while Nuriye and I examined her latest weaving, the men spoke of men's business. She was weaving her tapestry in patterns of reds and blues to keep her home warm.

"I hope Abram will set up my loom when we have a home," I said. "I miss weaving and its calming effects."

"If he does not, I have an extra I can share with you," Nuriye said.

"That would be wonderful," I said. "But first, I need to have a home beyond the Rose and Thorn Inn."

"That is a pleasant inn, but not a home."

"No. But it will work until we find a home."

When we rejoined them, Meir said, "I believe we have found a home for you, Sarai. Our old neighbor has moved away to live with his children, who left Harran. His home and barns are empty."

Abram's eyes lit up as he tucked me under his arm.

"Your neighbor?" I asked.

"That would be lovely," Nuriye said. "We will be neighbors. That is a nice home, although old Erim did not keep it as clean as you would like in his old age. I will bring my servant to come to help you clean it."

"I would love to live next to you, but clean?" I shuddered. "Any vermin?"

"No. None that I have seen," Nuriye said. "I do not like vermin, either. No one has lived in that house for some time. It is dusty. You will want to clean it before you bring your possessions in."

"Who do I have to speak to before I claim it?" Abram asked with a grin and squeezing me.

"I believe the man is still in the city. I will find out tomorrow morning and send you a message. That will give our wives a day to rest before they are called on to clean that house," Meir said.

We visited more that evening before Abram and I left for the Rose and Thorn Inn.

"How will you return to the Inn?" Nuriye asked. "Kadir has taken his carriage and gone."

"I will take Sarai with me on my horse, Smoke," Abram said. "We have often ridden like this in Ur."

"I love to hold on to him from behind," I said. *I enjoy feeling his muscles beneath my hands. I always feel safe with him.*

"The thieves will be out soon," Nuriye said. "Be safe."

"I will. I am prepared," Abram said.

I nodded and fingered the hilt of my belt knife. "Thieves will not take me."

Abram mounted Smoke, then offered me his hand. He lifted me onto the back of the horse and waited while I settled my skirts around me.

"Are you ready?" he asked.

"I am."

We bid our new friends farewell. "I look forward to living close to Nuriye," I said as we rode out their gate.

"It will be good for you to have a friend."

He turned toward the empty house, riding past so I could see. "Will it be big enough?"

I stared at the small house built like all the others in Harran. Not as large as our home in Ur, but it would be ours, not Terah's. It would hold us and Terah, and our servants and animals. I suspected Lot and Galya would find a home to live in near us as well. Galya would appreciate a home of her own, as I would.

Abram turned Smoke back toward the center of Harran. The horse's hooves clopped through the almost empty streets. It surprised me that Abram could readily find our inn. He had not watched through a window as Kadir took us in his carriage.

"How do you know how to get back to the Rose and Thorn?" I asked.

"I have been in this city before and know where I am," Abram said. "Besides, I have an excellent sense of direction. We will arrive there soon."

I watched for thieves in every direction, my heart beating faster than normal, sure they would attack us. "As long as no one attacks."

"Fear not, Sarai. We will arrive safely." He patted my hands clinging to him.

He turned the horse down another street. Soon I saw the signboard announcing the Rose and Thorn Inn and breathed a sigh of relief.

"You did it," I said.

"You doubted me," he chuckled softly. "I have been to Meir's home before. His shop is behind the house. I have traveled many times between his home and the Rose and Thorn."

My laugh was shaky in relief.

As we reached the gate, a servant pulled it open enough to allow us through. Abram brought Smoke to a stop and helped me slip off the horse's back. Abram soon followed.

"Come with me while I care for Smoke, then we can go inside together."

"I can go inside alone."

"Yes, you could, but I prefer you stay with me. I want no more surprises."

I nodded and shuddered as I remembered waking to a silent fight outside my door. I did not want another priest's man to come looking for me.

"Will we be safe here in Harran?" I asked, following Abram into bright the barn. Our servants had hung lit lanterns for us.

"Until the priests learn they cannot take us, I want you to stay close to me, or have our servants guard our door." He scooped oats into a trough and grabbed the curry brush.

"Do you trust all our servants? One of them could be the one who marked our tent."

Abram stopped brushing the horse and frowned at me. "How can I not trust them? They left their homes behind, bringing their families with them."

"Or to be a spy for the priests? We already had one of the priest's men stop at our door." I folded my arms tight across my body as I watched him.

Abram pulled a bit of his beard into his mouth and chewed on it while he brushed his horse. At last, he spit out the bit of his beard. "I will find a way to determine which of our servants, if any, betrayed us."

"And? Then what will you do if you discover one?"

"Send him back to Ur and to the priests. They will give them an appropriate punishment." Abram put the brush away and led Smoke to the trough and filled it with water.

After the horse finished drinking, we took him to his stall and closed the gate. Abram took my hand and pulled me close to walk with him inside. "I take care of my horse so he will take care of me. I take care of you and protect you because I love you. You are precious to me."

The following afternoon, we received word that Erim, the owner of the home next to Meir and Nuriye, would sell it to us. Although the Rose and Thorn was comfortable, it was an inn, not a home.

The herders took our sheep and goats to our new home and settled them in their new pastures. Our little group put on our traveling clothing and rode our camels with them.

Abram unlocked the door and pushed it open. We bumped into each other and stepped back, giggling and waiting for the others in our rush to enter and see our new home.

Although it looked small from the outside, the inside was spacious, with room for everyone. Servants' quarters had been attached to the back, so even Ela, Nitza, and Yitzhak and his family had a place to sleep.

Galya and Lot accepted a room in our home. "For now," she said. "I want this blessing for me too. A home I can live in and love. It does not have to be large, but it needs to be mine."

Lot pulled her into a hug. "We will find a home for us."

Over the next few days, my friends and our servants helped me brush away the cobwebs, sweep away the dirt, and wash everything in our new home. We made it ready to move into a welcoming and warm home.

After we moved in, we went through our clothing and other possessions, shaking out the dust and cleaning them. I wanted to be free of the dust and dirt of the trail.

At last I could sit back and enjoy my home. My home. I never thought I would have a home that did not belong to Abram's mother. Now, to fill it with the children Jehovah promised.

I walked through the house and decided where to locate the children's room. I dreamed of many children and hoped to need many beds for them all. Boys and girls, enough to need a room for each.

"Look what I found," Abram said.

I turned and saw him carrying my loom. "In our hurry to leave Ur, I did not remember packing it," I said as I threw my arms round his neck and hugged him close to me.

"I knew you would want to make tapestries and blankets for our home."

He set it up in the corner of the small workroom I had claimed.

"I will begin weaving right away," I said. "Thank you. Thank Jehovah. I never expected a home like this when we raced away from Ur."

He pulled me into his arms and held me close. "I have wanted to give you a home for years. I am grateful for you."

"It was the custom to live with your parents."

"And I could have built an addition in the —" He sunk in the chair in front of my loom and pulled me onto his lap.

"No. Your mother needed you near. She needed your help." I nuzzled his neck.

"She did, as did Father and the others. But you deserved a home."

"Now I have a home, and your father and nephew." I leaned back to gaze into his face filled with love and compassion.

"Lot and Galya will move out soon. He is looking for a home close by. You would not know what to do without having her close."

I snuggled close to him in his lap. "It would be nice to find out. Nuriye lives next door and is becoming a wonderful friend. Where will your father stay, with us or with Lot?"

Abram kissed me. "He will probably stay with us. I am the son."

"Yes. I suspected he would. I will still be mistress of our home and I will be happy."

He hugged me close. "Father will be happy to be in your home. You have treated him well."

"I have loved your father, only —" I stopped speaking, not wanting to say the words.

"Only you do not trust him."

I shook my head against his chest. "Not after what he did in Ur. I know he has apologized. But ..." My voice trailed off.

"But he has lost our trust," he whispered.

"Yes," I whispered.

"We will be watchful. He will not send us to be sacrificed again. It cannot happen again."

"How can you stop him?" I leaned back to see the truth in his eyes.

"Jehovah will protect us."

I nodded. "He has always protected us. He saved you from the sacrificial knife in Ur."

"He has promised us blessings. Trust Jehovah."

Tears leaked from my eyes. "I trust Jehovah to protect us. I do not trust Terah."

Abram pulled me back close. "If we keep him close, we can ensure he does not easily fall into the control of any temple priests here. I will work to keep him busy."

We sat together for a long time before I pushed away and stood. "You set my loom up for me. Now I can get busy creating a tapestry for the wall."

"What will you use as your design?"

I wanted to string the long warp threads on the loom. I needed to find them. "Not people. Jehovah has taught us not to worship idols or images. I need to think of a design without those."

"Why not include the stars we see at night?" Abram suggested.

"I like that idea. I'll have to spend some time outside, remembering where they are."

"And I can help you remember. I love the stars."

I found the warp threads in a basket and started stringing the warp threads, preparing for the weft and the pattern. "I know you love the stars. I do, too."

Galya and Lot poked their heads into the door of my workroom. "Here you are," she said.

"Abram set up my loom for me. I am starting a new tapestry to help remember our trip here," I said, grinning at her.

"Lot has found a home for us. We will move into it in three days," Galya said, her voice squeaking in excitement.

"Three days? I will have you here with me for only three more days? Will you need our help to clean it?"

"I will be down the road, not far. It is the third house down the street. There is some dust inside, but it is not as dirty as this one was. Nitza and I can clean it." Galya pressed her lips together in a slight grimace. "I do not know why, but the houses are empty on this end of the city."

"Empty?" My eyebrows crunched together. "Why are these houses emptying? What has happened here that the people are leaving?" I turned my stare to Abram.

He rolled his eyes upward. "I have not heard. I will ask Meir. He will know. I wondered why Erim asked so little for this house," he said.

"I am not complaining about the cost of the house," Lot said. "We do not have extra coins for a home. But this price was too good to pass up."

I fixed my stare on Abram. "Why would these houses cost so little?"

"I will discover the truth," Abram said, leaving the room.

"I do not mind," Galya said. "I finally get a home. I did not think I would have one for years."

I put my arm around her waist. "I did not expect a home even now. We are both blessed because we followed Jehovah's directions. Obedience brought us the blessing of having a home now."

"I know. I am sorry you and Abram suffered such a scare. How can you be so calm? I would still be afraid of any stranger." She brushed her hair back from her face.

I continued adding warp threads to my loom. "And you think I am not? I fear every stranger will try to drag Abram back to Ur." I shuddered. "I have to trust Jehovah and Abram."

"You are stronger than me. I would still be weeping in a corner."

"No, you would not. You are strong and would do what you must, to be with your Lot."

"You are right, I would. I have done much already to be with my Lot."

I nodded. "We all have."

Chapter Six

Thieves

"You will never believe why so many people are leaving this part of Harran," Abram said that evening as we prepared for bed.

My dress fell to the floor in a puddle at my feet before I stooped to pick it up. "What is the problem with this part of town?"

"Thieves. They wait near the wells and chase away the sheep while the herder draws water from the well. Too many lost their herds to the thieves."

I gasped. First idolatrous priest intent on sacrificing us and now thieves. "That is not good. We do not have enough sheep and goats to allow thieves to drive them away. What will you do about them?"

"Now that we know, Lot and I will take our herders with us to the well. We will go in greater strength than the thieves."

I glanced up at Abram. "You will stay safe?"

"You know I will. I did not bring you here to leave you alone. We will be careful." He pulled me into his arms and held me tight. "I will do my part and depend on Jehovah to continue to defend me."

"It is all I can ask for."

The next day I was skittish, struggling to stay focused on my tasks while Abram and Lot were gone. They had left early with the herders, hoping to avoid the thieves. Jehovah would bless them, but I still feared he could be injured.

I started weaving my tapestry with dark blue threads from my supply. Abram and I had stood in the back of our home gazing into the night sky, setting into our memory the placement of each star. Then we set them on a sheet of vellum as a pattern.

I planned to use the dark blue for the night sky and bits of white for the stars. I wove a few rows, then wandered to the front of the house and peeked out the window, hoping to see Abram and the others returning with the animals. Each time I peered out, I chastised myself. *I know Jehovah will protect him. Why am I worried? But they are thieves. Oh, Jehovah, bless my Abram.*

Finally, as the sun began to fall toward the west, and after many trips to the front window and many chastisements, I heard bleating in the road outside. I ran to the window and saw our herders walking back with our animals. Abram walked in the lead, followed by the sheep.

I ran to the back door and pulled it open. I hurried to lean against the wall near where the men would take the animals for the night, arriving in time to watch Abram lead them through the gate and back to the paddocks. Bleating sheep and goats followed him, along with Lot and the herders.

Abram walked tall, his shepherd's crook stabbing the dirt with each step. His grim face and stiff posture told me something had happened. My muscles tightened. What?

I stood beside the wall along the edge of the path, counting the animals as they passed. They represented our future. They trusted Abram as he trusted Jehovah.

All the animals were there. They had lost none. What happened at the well?

I breathed deeply to calm my mind. I needed to trust Jehovah as Abram did. He promised safety. We had to trust Him.

Galya touched my arm. "The men are home safely. Why have you been so restless today?"

Grateful they had not moved into their new home yet, I shook my head. I did not know what she knew. "Did Lot tell you?"

"He did. Thieves have been stealing animals at the well. I have been worried about them."

"Did they bring all the animals back?"

I nodded mutely.

"I did not see any signs of our men needing to fight."

"Perhaps they did not, but Abram does not look happy."

Together we watched the animals enter the safety of the paddock. After a time, the men left. Abram and Lot strode toward us.

"Something must have happened," she whispered. "He is glowering."

"Yes. I never want to see that look after I do something dumb."

"What is going on?" Lot asked as they neared us. "You never meet us when we return with the goats and sheep."

Galya lifted a shoulder. "I searched for Sarai to tell her something and found her out here. Did you have a nice day with the animals?"

"Interesting," Lot said.

I watched Abram's face. I doubted he would describe the day that way.

"It was a day," he said.

He took my arm with a tenseness similar to the day in Ur and walked with me toward the house in silence. I could hear Galya chattering to Lot behind us but did not focus on her words. I was worried about the thieves and what Abram had done.

We walked through the house and up the stairs to our rooms, where he finally released my arm with a heavy sigh.

"What happened out there?" I asked, stepping behind him to rub his shoulders.

He dropped into a chair and groaned. "It was as Meir warned. The thieves waited in the bushes while we prepared to water the animals. Azar had emptied a third bucket of water into the water trough when three thieves stepped out from the bushes. Lot, the other herders, and I were ready. We had arranged ourselves in a circle defending the herd so we could stop them from running. They still ran a distance before we could gather them all back in. The thieves were not happy."

I kneaded his shoulders like I kneaded bread. "Your shoulders are as hard as boulders. What did the thieves do?"

"They lifted their swords as if they wanted to fight us, but with so many of us and so few of them, they slipped away and disappeared into the bushes."

"They had become too confident they could steal animals by driving them away."

Abram slumped in his chair. His muscles had not relaxed yet. I continued to push and rub them.

"They have. I fear they will bring more men with them tomorrow. I do not want to fight them. Jehovah teaches we should not kill."

"They must be ferocious if all the other herders in this area have left." I squeezed his back muscles. They slowly loosened.

"These were not. I expected them to be more savage. Perhaps because they only brought three men, they did not expect us to fight back. I had hoped to start selling our wool to the local weavers, but until we solve the matter with the thieves, I cannot."

"Can Lot handle the thieves?" I used my knuckles on a knot in his shoulder.

He moaned in relief. "Not yet. These thieves need to be fearful of me and my men."

Each day for two weeks, Abram and Lot went with the herders. Each day they returned tired from gathering the scattered sheep and goats each morning and night. Lot put off the move into their new home until the problem was solved.

"We have enough herders to prevent the loss of any animals," Abram said one evening as I once again massaged the knots from his shoulders, "but one day, they will succeed. They will take one or more of our animals."

"What will you do?"

Abram shook his head. "Continue to water the animals and guard them from thieves. Their numbers grow, making it more difficult to safeguard our herd."

"Will they force you to fight?" I asked from behind him as I worked on a tight muscle.

"This must end. I cannot pay them to go away. It would only bring more out to get easy coins. I have prayed about this, but still have not discovered a way to end it."

"They may force you to fight them."

Abram sagged in his chair. "I know. I do not want to kill any of them."

I stopped meeting them along the path to the paddocks. Abram would come to me after they had bedded down the animals for the night. He did not need me to show concern for his safety in front of his men.

Galya and Nitza finished cleaning her new home and began moving in. It took them longer than they expected, since securing the sheep from thieves kept Lot and our herders busy.

Then one day, the men returned early. The sun had just reached its zenith when I heard the bleating of the sheep and goats.

I hurried out the door and to the path to see why they had returned so early. Galya joined me by the wall near the end of the path, watching our men stride toward us, their backs stiff and their shepherd's crooks pounding into the dirt.

"Something happened," I whispered.

"Yes," she said. "Look at their robes. They are torn."

A rip ran from the neck down the back of Abram's robe. The arm holes of Lot's robe had torn. Something had rent Terah's robe almost into two pieces. All the other herders had tears in their robes. The men paraded past us without glancing in our direction. I knew Abram saw us. He saw everything.

"When did Terah join the herders?" I asked.

"Lot said something last night about Terah planning to go with them today."

I groaned. Terah was not known for his patience and calm.

The animals scampered past, following behind Abram. He had often led them out to green pastures and brought them home safely. Even though he hired men to help, his sheep and goats followed him, knowing he would defend them.

I coughed in the dust that the animals stirred up and turned away from them.

Galya grabbed my arm. "Look at Azar."

I pulled my headscarf across my face and turned back to watch Azar and the others limp past me. Two herders held up a third.

What had happened this morning to injure our men?

Galya echoed my thoughts.

I could only shake my head. "We will learn when our men tell us."

The wives of the herders had joined us near the wall. Now they hurried out the gate, following their men to the animal paddocks. They would care for their men as we would care for ours.

I waited with Galya by the gate. Abram and Lot would return to us when they had the animals and men settled. Galya shifted her feet and harrumphed, impatient for them to return and share the story.

The men would come to us when they were ready. No amount of rocking on her feet or harrumphing would hurry them. I watched her with a little smile. She and Lot had not been married as long as Abram and I had. She would learn.

It seemed like an eternity before our men finally shambled toward us, their exhaustion apparent in their sagging faces and limping feet.

Galya could wait no longer. She ran to Lot and threw her arms around him.

"Ouch, Galya. That hurts," Lot moaned.

I sighed as she dropped her arms. He must have received injuries in ways that did not show. Tears streaked in the dust on her face as she and Lot passed us. Terah crunched his eyebrows together and nodded toward them as he slouched behind them.

Abram's arms surrounded me and pulled me close.

"Will I not hurt you?" I asked.

"I need to feel you near me after —," he said.

"What happened?"

"Father." Abram almost spat out the word.

"What did he do?" We ambled behind the others toward the house.

Abram shook his head. "Not now. In the privacy of our rooms. I cannot say it where others may hear." His arm tightened.

I nodded. "How badly were you hurt?"

"Not as much as I could have been, but more than I should have. It was not a good situation." He rolled his lips inward and pressed them together.

What had Terah done this time? Before the incident with the priests of Elkenah caused us to flee Ur, we could trust him to have common sense. Had he changed that much?

Abram sighed heavily as we neared the house door. "Be patient, dear. I will share everything when we are certain of our privacy."

We entered and walked through the house without speaking. In our suite of rooms, Ela had filled the tub with hot, steaming water. A thick towel and washing cloth sat on the stool beside the tub. A bar of sweet-smelling soap sat in a dish on the edge.

"Be sure to thank Ela for me," Abram said as he stripped off his robe and tunic. I gasped as he stepped into the hot water with a sigh.

Large, purple bruises covered much of his body and thighs.

"I thought you said you had only a few injuries," I said.

"I said I had not as many as I could, but more than I should. My body hurts." He tried to look at his back with a groan. "How bad are the bruises?"

I traced the large purple bruises on his back with a gentle finger. "Here, here, and here are the biggest. There are more little ones here," I traced a smaller bruise, "and here. Bruises cover much of your back. They cross over in some places."

Abram leaned back in the tub and closed his eyes. "I expected worse. I am blessed to have only the bruises."

"What happened? Why are you so injured?"

Abram's eyes stayed closed for a long time before they finally opened. "You should sit."

I moved the towel to a chair and picked up the washing cloth before I sat on the stool beside the tub. I dipped it into the water and rubbed it on the bar of soap.

"Let me help you wash while you tell me your story," I said, taking his arm and washing it.

"I can wash myself," Abram argued, dropping his arm beneath the water.

"You can, but you have a story to tell me, and I need to have something to do while you share. It will be hard to hear. I can tell."

He lifted his arm from the water and held it out for me. "Father decided he would go with us today to help us solve our problem with the thieves. At one time, he could resolve conflicts with ease. But since he fell under the control of the Priests of Elkenah, he has lost all sensibility."

I washed his arm, set it in the water, then lifted his other arm to wash. "I have noticed his tendency to choose anger more often."

Abram nodded. "I hesitated when he told me he planned to join us this morning. I even left the house early, hoping to be gone before he came out. But the animals were slow this morning, and Father joined us before they left the paddocks."

"Did he notice your effort to leave him behind?" I set his arm in the water and began to wash his chest.

"He did not say anything about us leaving him behind. He apologized for sleeping late. I only wish he had slept later."

"Oh," I said, trying not to stop the flow of Abram's words.

"We stop at the well on our way to the pastures each morning. We have surrounded the herd, preventing them from scattering. The thieves are growing tired of trying to take our animals from us. I had hoped that today would be the day they stopped trying."

I lifted one of his legs and washed it. He grunted in pain. "It was not?"

"Perhaps it is now. I suspect it would have come to the results we had today, but I did not want it to happen the way it did."

My cloth stopped at his knee. "What happened?"

Abram sighed and closed his eyes. "They have been gathering larger numbers of men each day, making it difficult to frighten them off. Father decided he would resolve the problem today his way."

"Yes, you said that." I set his leg in the tub and lifted the other one.

"Father chose to confront them and told us to hold the animals back from the well so he could call out to them." He sighed again. "I did not like it, but he is my father ... He went ahead, with Lot and I following. It was as bad as I expected."

I set his leg in the tub and asked him to lean forward so I could reach his back. "What did they do?"

"Father called them cheap cowards for hiding in the brush and waiting for us to arrive with our flocks. Men rushed from the bushes, many more men than the three of us could contend with. But Father would not stop his haranguing."

I set the cloth on the edge of the tub and listened. Each word filled me with more horror.

"I whispered to him they would attack us if he did not stop, but he looked at me with a grin. 'I want them to attack,' he said. I could not believe the glee in his voice. He was looking for a chance to fight."

Abram slammed his hand into the water, splashing it everywhere. I flinched back away from the splash, but it showered me. I grabbed his towel and wiped my face and hands off.

"I am sorry, Sarai, but Father makes me so angry sometimes. There was no need to entice them into a conflict. We could have solved it with no injuries."

His arm came down toward the water again and I leaned away from him. His arm slowed and the splash stayed in the tub.

"The men fought you?" I asked.

Abram nodded. "They could not accept Father's affronts. They ran at us with swords raised."

"And you all still live?"

"Our men do, only because Jehovah preserved us. He probably should not have, with Father shouting at them the way he did. Our herders joined the fray, attacking from behind and bringing our numbers of men closer to the number of men against us."

I pinched my lips together to keep from saying anything. It would not help to voice my opinion of Terah at that moment.

"Yes," Abram said. "I did not like the situation, but I was in the middle of it, swinging my staff to keep the men away. I hit them hard, some on the side of the head. When one fell, I looked for another to fight. We fought for nearly an hour before the thieves who still remained on their feet ran away, leaving their friends behind."

I dropped the hand I had put my hand to my mouth during his narration. "Did you kill any of them?"

"I did not want to. I know three had broken arms, two had broken legs. One did not move when his friends returned to drag him away. I do not know if he still lives."

"And all our men are safe?"

Abram nodded. "We all have bruises. Some have cuts from the thieves' swords."

I stiffened. Another thought frightened me. "Will it cause us to be sent from Harran?"

Abram sank below the surface of the water and came out in a splash. "I do not know. Will you wash my hair for me as well?"

I picked up the soap and rubbed it on my hands until I had enough to wash his hair. His sighs of relief, with an occasional yelp when I found another injury, accompanied the movement of my hands over his head. I wanted to scream at Terah.

"I do not think we killed anyone. Only one did not move during all the time we watered our flocks. We brought the flocks home early, rather than wait for a reaction from the thieves and their friends."

"What will tomorrow bring?" I asked.

"I do not know. I hope they stop trying to take our animals."

Chapter Seven

Traitor

For much of the next day, I worried the thieves would attack Abram and the herders again. I struggled to keep my mind at ease and focus on the work I had set for myself. I would have gone out to help Ela and Nitza wash the clothing, but I knew they would chase me away.

I wandered from my loom to the window to a seat in the sitting room where I kept a basket of mending. Nothing could keep my mind busy enough. Worry continued to plague me.

As the sun neared setting, I heard the animals bleating as they trotted down the path. Our men had come home. I rushed out the back door to the wall to watch our men stride down the path ahead of the sheep and goats. Galya soon joined me, watching the parade of animals and herders jostling each other down the path to the paddocks. None were injured. I breathed a sigh of relief and turned toward the house.

"Where are you going?" Galya asked, surprise filling her voice. "I thought you would wait for the men to finish with the animals."

I smiled. "No need. They are safe. I can go back to my work. Abram will come tell me what happened today when he has fed and bedded the animals, as he always does."

"But yesterday—"

"Was yesterday. Today is different. I can see they are all well and happy. He can share after they care for the animals." I turned and strode into the house.

Ela and Nitza had the table set for the family and the evening meal nearly ready. So I settled on a comfortable chair in our main sitting room and waited for Abram.

Galya did not stand by the wall for long. She entered the room, sat in a comfortable chair across from mine, and picked up her mending.

"We will move to our home soon. The herders will not need Lot every day now, since the animals are safely going to feed and water."

I let Abram's tunic I was mending fall to my lap. "I will miss you, Galya. We have been together for many years."

"I will miss you, and I know Nitza will miss Ela, but we will only be down the street, not in another city or land."

"That is true. And Lot will continue to help Abram with the animals."

"He will help to sell the wool from them as well. We will stay close."

"When do you think you will go?"

Galya stabbed her needle through the seam and pulled it out. "If all is well, I believe we will go the day after tomorrow."

"That soon? I hoped you would stay another week at least."

"I did not unpack everything, so it will not take long to get our possessions ready to move."

"It would not. I hope you are happy in your new home."

"It is like this one, with the tall roof. We will be cool and comfortable. We will keep a room for Grandfather Terah for those days you grow tired of him."

"As if anyone would tire of me," Terah said as he entered the sitting room. He plopped into Abram's favorite seat and grinned.

"Indeed," I said, laughter filling my voice, but I nodded my thanks to Galya. There would be times we would need to rest from him.

Abram and Lot entered soon after. Abram glanced at his father, sitting in his seat, then seated himself in the chair beside mine. He briefly pinched his lips together. "What are you mending today, Sarai?"

"Your tunic. You tore it in your battles with the thieves."

"No more torn tunics for us," Terah crowed. "We frightened them away yesterday."

My eyebrows raised and I turned to Abram.

"No thieves met us at the well today," Lot agreed, sitting near Galya. "Perhaps they have learned a lesson."

"After one day, you believe they are gone?" Abram asked, staring at his father and nephew."

"They did not come back today," Terah said. "We frightened them away."

"For today. Maybe even for tomorrow," Abram said, leaning forward in his chair. "I do not expect they will stay gone. Wait until they heal from their injuries."

"Ha! We frightened them away. They will not be back."

"I do not know, Grandfather," Lot said. "One day with no thieves is nice, but I suspect we will always need to be wary of them."

Abram nodded and leaned back. "They will return when they think we have become complacent. It will not happen. We will always be watchful."

Terah shook his head. "You two are whining women. Those thieves will not return."

"I hope not, but we need to stay alert. One time would be all they need to steal our flocks," Lot said.

During their discussion, I completed the needed repair on Abram's tunic, folded it, and set it in my lap. *Abram is right. He is not a whining woman, he is careful of our safety and the safety of our animals.*

"Shall we go put my tunic away?" Abram asked, standing and offering me his hand.

"Yes. Dinner will be ready soon. Ela and Nitza will be waiting for us."

We left the others and climbed the stairs to the privacy of our suite.

"Is it over?" I asked as I hung his tunic on a peg.

"No. As I told Father and Lot, we will need to stay alert to the thieves. But today was a good day. All the animals were watered and taken to the pastures to eat with no problems. I pray Jehovah helps us do this every day."

I stepped into his arms. "I hope we can be happy here in Harran. Perhaps Jehovah will open my womb." My hand touched my stomach, yearning.

"It would be wonderful if He did. He promised us many children," Abram said, nuzzling my neck.

I kissed him tenderly. The promise did not stop my desire for children to come soon. Then the dinner bell echoed through the house. "But now is not the time for that," I said, stepping away. "Ela and the others are waiting for us."

"We do not want Father asking why we are late," Abram said, reluctantly letting me go. "But later ..."

"Yes, later," I agreed, grinning at the thought.

He quickly changed from his dirty tunic and washed his face, arms, and hands before we left our rooms and strolled down to the dinner table.

The thieves did not attack again for many months. In that time, Galya and Lot moved into their own home. Abram took samples of the wool from our animals into the city and many dyers and weavers agreed to purchase lots of wool from him.

When the thieves finally attacked again, our men were ready, fighting them off once more. Our men returned bruised and battered as they had after the first battle, but they hurt the thieves worse. They sallied out occasionally to see if our men had dropped their guards, but they never did. Eventually, the thieves gave up.

The next years were comfortable. I completed my tapestry and began another. Abram used my tapestry often to teach others of the stars. I learned much as I listened in.

The animals were happy, and our herds increased in size. With so many, others considered Abram to be a wealthy man.

Once more, we taught our friends of Jehovah. Some listened and accepted baptism. We met often with them as we worshiped Jehovah. Each month, however, Abram comforted me when my womb continued to refuse to hold a child within it.

"Are you certain you do not want to put me away or take another wife? Perhaps I am not the one to mother your children," I would cry bitterly.

He embraced me each time while I cried. "I chose you to be my wife. I do not want someone else. I want you. A child will come."

I tried to believe him. I tried to trust Jehovah would send us a child, but each month was a disappointment. Each month Abram held me close and soothed away my fears and disappointment.

News arrived that Ur was suffering a debilitating drought. People deserted the city, seeking to find a home in a place where there was sufficient water. Harran grew, bringing followers of the religions of Ur. Once more, Abram kept me close, wanting to defend me from the danger of their priests.

The people of Harran had overused the wells, and no rains replenished them. Harran, too, now suffered a drought.

Terah slipped out in the evening, unwilling to share where he went. "I am a grown man. I can go out in the evening," he would argue.

Abram growled under his breath, but Terah was correct. He could come and go as he pleased. I noticed the odor of strong wine on his breath on mornings after he stayed out late. I could neither say nor do nothing about it.

"I fear he has returned to the influence of those who worship idols," Abram said to me one evening. "He refuses to join us in evening prayers to Jehovah."

I brushed my hair as my usual preparation for sleep. "What will you do?"

Abram shrugged and dropped heavily onto the bed. "Pray he does not find a reason to have us sacrificed again."

"He would not do that," I cried, my brush poised in the air above my hair. "Would he? Did he not learn in Ur?"

Abram ran his hands through his hair. "I do not know. How can he return to Elkenah?"

"It is like a dog returning to his vomit." I returned to brushing my hair.

Abram stood behind me and took my brush. I let him brush my hair, relaxing under his gentle ministrations. He brushed my hair for a time before saying anything else.

"We may have to leave him here in Harran —"

"Leave our home? But you and Lot are doing well." I tried to control the screech in my voice. My head jerked, snagging the brush in my hair and pulling it from Abram's hands. I loved this home.

"We knew we would be here for only a time," Abram said, recapturing the brush and moving it through my hair. "I have received word from Jehovah once more. We are to leave Harran."

"Oh?" My voice caught in my throat. I did not expect him to hear from Jehovah again. What had he asked of us this time?

"He has a purpose for us to minister in a strange land. We are to take Lot and leave."

"When?" I bit my lip, waiting for the answer.

"We have time to gather our possessions and our flocks. But we cannot stay much longer."

"And Terah?" I held my breath as I awaited his answer.

Abram sucked in a breath. "He will stay here in Harran."

"You will leave him behind?"

"Yes. He no longer believes in Jehovah, and I cannot trust him."

The brush continued to move through my hair, soothing me.

"So, when do we leave?" I eventually asked.

"We have a week. Can you be ready in that time?"

I thought through everything I would need to do. There was washing our clothing, packing, disassembling my loom, getting the tapestry I currently wove to a stopping place, and so many more chores. "I can do it, but I will need to work long hours to get things ready. What about those others who have learned to believe in Jehovah? Will you be leaving them here or take them with us?"

"I hope they will travel with us. It is easier to worship Jehovah in larger groups, and I do not want to lose these people to the priests of Elkenah."

"No, we cannot have that. When will you talk to them?"

"We meet to worship tomorrow morning. I will invite them to join us in our travels."

I nodded. "They will want to be invited. I hope they all join us." I covered a yawn. "It has been a long day. I am tired."

"Our next days will be busy," Abram said, leading me to the bed.

As I lay in his arms in the dark, he continued to share. "Jehovah told me more."

"Oh?" I asked, yawning again.

"We will be blessed. Jehovah told me He would make of us a great nation."

"What does that mean?" I murmured.

"Our children will have many children."

"Our children?" I said with a small gasp. "We have no children."

"No yet, but we will." Abram kissed me. "We will."

Jehovah promises us children, but every month I am disappointed. How can our family become a great nation if my womb is not opened? What have I done wrong? What must I do to receive this gift?

When invited, most of our little group of Jehovah worshippers agreed to travel with us. Abram supplied those who had little means with tents and an opportunity to join our herders. Everyone gathered their available food. We added all we could to our supplies of dwindling food caused by the drought, knowing we would feed many people.

Abram quietly gave the men coins to purchase tents, camels, and donkeys. He did not want the leaders of Harran to know of his leaving.

We had hoped for Meir and Nuriye to travel with us, but they chose to stay with their families.

"We can help ensure none of the priests' men follow you," Nuriye said. "And, we can help watch over Terah."

It saddened me to leave my friend, but it would be for the best. They were among the first to listen to Abram's teachings of the wonders of Jehovah.

Before we left, Galya, Nuriye, and I washed all our clothing, knowing it could be difficult to clean them as we traveled through the desert. Our servants, Ela and Nitza, prepared food to carry with us for a distance.

"Mistress," Ela said as we washed the clothing, "I have worked for you a long time."

"Yes," I replied. "You have. I have been grateful for your help."

"But now, Mistress," Ela stopped scrubbing the stain on one of Abram's tunics and frowned at me. "I have found a man who wants me as his wife. I wish to stay here in Harran with him."

"You found a man," Galya said. "Who is he?"

"Rahim. You would not know him. But he loves me and will take care of me."

I knew the name. Terah had spoken it in his drunken stupors. Not someone I would want Ela to join with. "Then stay here with him. Perhaps Terah will keep you on" I said. Thoughts raced through my head. *Who is this man? Why is she leaving me now when we are leaving? Who will take her place?* My ribs grew tight, restricting my breath. *After everything I have done for her?* My heart pounded. *Why?*

"Is Master Terah not going with you?" Nitza said.

"No," Galya said. "He says he is too old to travel such a long distance."

"I have already spoken to him," Ela said. "He will take us as his servants."

"Us?" I asked. "You and your new husband?"

"Yes," Ela said. "And Nitza and her new husband. She has a man now too."

"You too?" Galya cried, touching her throat. "What will I do without you, Nitza?"

Nitza playfully hit her sister on the arm. "I was to tell Galya, not you."

Ela shrugged, jutted out her chin, and continued to scrub the tunic.

"Jarom is a good man. I desire to be with him," Nitza said, dipping her chin. Red crept up her neck and over her face.

"I am certain Jarom is a good man, but who will help me?" Galya whined.

"We have others who will travel with us," I said. "Perhaps one will consent to help you."

"Do you think so?" Galya asked.

"I hope so. I will need the help of another woman myself," I said. *One I can trust. One I can train to serve me as I like, not like Ahuva wanted. It may be nice.*

We packed our baskets and bags with our clean clothing and possessions, preparing them to be tied to donkeys and camels. As I did, I thought through the list of women who would travel with us. Who would work for us? Who would accept the challenge of Galya? She had become less scattered in Harran, but she continued to take her time. Traveling could be difficult.

That evening when I told Abram about Ela and Nitza, he shook his head. "I have hoped my suspicions about Nitza were mistaken. But this Jarom came from Ur shortly after we did. I saw him speaking to the priests on the day of that last sacrifice. I fear we have found our traitor."

"But Jarom did not travel with us."

"No. But Nitza did. She refused to follow my guidance and lagged far behind the others in the windstorm."

"You think she did it on purpose?" I asked, allowing my eyes to widen.

"I have long wondered. I think she is the one they thought would mark our tent, or one who helped Jarom when he marked it."

I gasped. "We have kept a traitor with us all this time? Galya has loved her like a sister."

"I know, but I fear she is the one. She, or this Jarom. She moped around until after Jarom arrived in Harran. I suspect she thought he was among those caught in the windstorm."

I prayed for Jehovah's help in choosing the right woman. I did not want to offend one of His followers by asking one to help me, but I need help. Perhaps one of them would need my help as much as I needed hers.

Those followers of Jehovah, who had chosen to come with us, gathered the next day with their baskets and bags in our courtyard, bringing their possessions prepared to be loaded on the animals.

I cleared my throat and said, "Ela is not going with us. Neither she nor her sister, Nitza, will travel with us."

"You need servants, Mistress," Bara said. "You and Mistress Galya. We will find one of our own to help you." As a woman of wisdom and an early convert to Jehovah's love, the women looked up to her.

"I would appreciate that. I have always had someone to assist me."

"There are some among us who feel unable to travel because of their poverty," Bara said.

"But Abram has offered support for all —"

"Yes, but some ..."

"We cannot allow poverty and an unwillingness to accept help to keep them here. It will not be safe for them to stay. I will hire the women. Abram will hire the men. He will need help. Some of our herders have chosen to stay here in Harran."

After speaking with those who wished to travel with us, but did not have the means, I hired Yael and Galya hired Avi to help us. Abram hired their husbands to help as herders, confident they would care for our possessions and needs. He and Lot hired the other men to help with the animals.

Then, early on the morning after the Sabbath, when most of Harran's populace still slept, our men loaded bags and baskets. In a little more than an hour, we mounted our camels and moved out of the city and south, toward Canaan.

Chapter Eight

Sorrow

We left in the milky early morning light before dawn. My camel had a rolling gait that caused me some nausea that first day. It was past my monthly time, and Abram prayed that this would be the time for me to carry our child. I joined his fervent prayers, for I had been too long without a child in my womb and in my arms.

After the first day, the nausea abated, and I could ride in more comfort. Hope filled my soul, but I said nothing to anyone except Abram. I did not want the other women to have false hope for me. It had happened before.

We followed a well-worn trail southward and the days became monotonous. We rose early in the gray dawn to prepare for each day's travel. Our maidservants, Yael and Avi, insisted they prepare our morning meal while Galya and I dressed. They put dried meat and fruit in our packs and filled our water skins so we could eat and drink along the way. Before the sun set in deep purples and golds, Abram would call a halt to our travel, and the women joined to prepare a meal for everyone. After three weeks of this, my body hardened once more, and the ride no longer hurt.

One night I woke with severe cramping in my belly. I feared the worst, and tears quietly leaked from the sides of my eyes into my pillows. My hopes had begun to rise. Now they cringed with every cramp in my stomach. Abram woke to my moans. He held me close as he prayed for Jehovah to bless me. However, I began to bleed. I rushed out to the latrine the men had dug when we stopped.

Blood poured from my body. I sat in a crumpled heap, weeping great tears as hope melted away until Abram found me. He tenderly carried me back to our tent, cradled in his arms.

"You will get my blood on you," I wept.

"It does not matter. I will wash."

"But your clothing?"

"It will also wash."

He murmured comforting words as he laid me back on our bed, covered with an old blanket. I heard a scratching on the tent pole and Abram left to see who had come. Bara bustled into the tent, expressing her concern.

During the night, she cared for me as the cramps grew stronger, wiping my forehead with a cool damp cloth and speaking soothing words. Abram perched beside me, holding my hand.

Eventually, my body expelled the child, too young to live, too small to know if I had carried a son or a daughter. Bara wrapped it gently in a cloth and set it aside. She told me it would do me no good to look, though even today I wish I had.

Abram held my hand as Bara worked to clean my body and set absorbent moss between my legs to catch the blood that flowed. Silent tears gushed down my face, carrying with them my sorrow.

After she had cleaned me, Bara covered me with a clean blanket, lifted the little bundle of a child, and carried it out of the tent. As the tent door swished open, I saw golden colors heralding dawn. I turned my face from their beauty and wept bitterly. I had lost the only child to have taken residence in my womb.

Galya came in to share my sorrow, and I noticed a swollen belly I had not seen before.

"You carry a child," I said.

Galya nodded. "I kept the knowledge to myself, not wanting to cause you pain."

"You are blessed of Jehovah. Take care of yourself."

"You are not sad that I carry a child and you ..." Galya lifted her arms in grief.

"No. I am happy for you. Sad for myself."

"You will conceive again. It will happen for you."

"Jehovah has promised us children," Abram said. "Sarai will conceive and carry a child."

But will I carry it to birth and help it grow? I gripped his hand, holding to his belief, wanting to trust Jehovah. My faith in this blessing had shrunk to a tiny seed.

After Galya left, I stared at Abram's hands holding mine. "After all these years, I finally conceive … and I lose the babe. Jehovah must know something I do not."

"He knows all things. He knows you will conceive again," Abram said.

"Will I?"

He took me in his arms and held me close. "He has promised me. You will have children."

We stayed in camp for three days while I healed. Abram stayed near me most of the time, only leaving to give directions to Lot and the herders to care for our animals. I turned my sorrow to the walls of the tent and refused to eat. He spooned food into my reluctant mouth until I agreed to eat once more.

The evening of the third day, I paused near the tent door. "We cannot stay here. There is no water. You must plan to move on tomorrow."

"Are you well enough to travel?" Abram asked.

"I must be. We cannot stay here."

He nodded and left the tent, calling to the others and giving directions for preparations to move on the next morning. Bara came to keep me company, as she often did. She was a good friend who did not offer false hope.

The next morning, I sadly climbed onto the back of my camel. Abram surrounded me with pillows to cushion the ride. I wanted to hide in my tent forever, but I knew we must find water or everyone would die.

"We will not travel the whole day," he said as he kissed me.

"We must ride until we find another well or a stream of water," I reminded him.

"We have enough water for another day. If you are too uncomfortable, we will stop." He kissed me again before mounting and giving both his and mine the order to stand.

I closed my eyes tightly against the dizziness. My ride followed Abram's. When the spinning ended, I opened one eyelid barely enough for light to seep in.

No dizziness.

I allowed the other eye to open and looked at the scenery. As usual, Abram and I rode at the head of the caravan. Lot and Galya rode behind. The others followed, some on camels, donkeys, or horses, and our other animals and their herders in the back. Abram's horse, Smoke, walked with the donkeys and other horses. He carried no pack. Abram's men had packed his saddle and loaded it onto camels.

I gazed at the occasional tree. A small patch of tiny yellow, star-shaped flowers grew close to the ground. How could there be such beauty in the desert when my heart was breaking? How could I, like the wilderness, find joy in my childless life?

But they grew in small patches, beside tiny blue flowers. My soul lifted toward heaven. If these flowers could grow in the desert, I could survive the loss of our only child. I could find bright patches of light to carry me through.

Abram stopped early that day when he found a small stream flowing from the mountains. Gratefully, I slid off and slumped into the shade of a tree. We rested and filled our water containers.

The next morning we left later than usual and stopped earlier. Abram rode beside me, but I barely noticed my surroundings, as I was lost in my sorrow. I wanted to be like Galya with a growing stomach, planning where to place the tiny bed in our tent, thinking of toys to keep the child happy. But, no. My arms and my womb were empty. Devoid of new life.

Bara and the other women came to me, offering hope and love. I appreciated their efforts but found my grief too deep for their love to touch.

Galya came to help, but her growing belly brought me to tears. She stayed away for many days, allowing Yael and Bara to care for my needs instead..

Abram held me through the night, his tears mingling with mine. But he had to be stoic during the day as he led our caravan along the road toward Damascus.

"We will stop in Damascus to allow you to rest longer," he said on the third evening of renewed travel.

"Is that safe?" I asked.

"We will need to resupply, but I do not believe we should stay long. Perhaps we can find others in that city who believe in Jehovah."

"It would be nice to sleep inside a city and not have to worry about bandits," I agreed.

"Bandits and thieves are everywhere. More in the cities than in the wilderness," he reminded me.

"We will have to be watchful, then."

We saw the gray, sturdy, stone walls of Damascus two days before we finally arrived at the city gates. They beckoned us like a strumpet on a street corner, promising safety and opportunity. I listened with little interest as Yael chattered about the sweets and fresh fruits to be found in the market. Jehovah had reproved me. Why had he not allowed me to carry this child? What had I done to be unworthy?

I did not share my concerns with Abram. He had too many other challenges as we moved along the trail. They had to be more watchful for thieves as we neared the city.

"They leave the safety of the city to come prey on travelers," he explained to me when I asked about it.

We rode past the remnants of a small caravan, destroyed by thieves. Even I became more alert, watching for signs of attackers. I wished I had learned to use a weapon better than my belt knife. Even a shepherd's crook would be helpful in an attack. But I had no strength to swing one, and Abram promised he would protect me and the other women if an attack came.

Even though we brought large herds of animals with us, our men bristled with weapons. Perhaps that protected us. More likely, Jehovah did. I did not think of Him protecting us then, but now, as I remember that time, He enfolded us in His protective arms.

Guards at the gate assumed we were coming to sell our animals and directed us toward the market. Abram bowed and thanked them for the information, then led us the way he suggested before taking us in another direction.

"Will the guards not be suspicious?" I asked, slowly recovering from my grief.

"They would be, but I followed their directions until we were out of their sight. We will need to be near the market to resupply, but we do not want to entice thieves with the size of our flocks."

"Where are you leading us?"

"I am led by the Lord. I will find a safe place for us and our flocks."

My camel followed his, led by a guide rope, as it had done since I lost our child and the energy to guide it or even care which way it went. Many herds of animals had bedded down near the walls of the city. I reclined in the comfort of the cushions surrounding me, only marginally wondering where Abram would take us.

He bypassed the men who tried to entice us into their paddocks nearest the wall with promises of safety and food, and continued along the wide street. It circled inside through the sludge of filth thrown from the windows into the streets.

I rubbed my nose, trying to wipe away the stench, then pulled my headscarf over my face. Even that did not block the stink.

Abram turned, then turned again, never looking back to see if the others followed. I turned to see Lot had fallen to the rear to help keep the animals together and protect them from theft.

The wide, winding roads narrowed, and I shivered as tall buildings blocked out the warmth of the sun. I peered upward to see only a small patch of blue pushing between the rooftops. I shuddered, more from fear of the unknown than the cold.

Abram must have sensed my fear, for he urged our company to move faster, pushing throngs of people to the edges of the street and ignoring their cries and curses.

We turned another corner onto a wider street. Abram brought his camel to a stop. Mine stopped beside his.

"Where are we?" I asked.

He pointed to the signboard above the entrance to a building. It read "Mahdi's Inn and Tavern."

"This looks safe?" I said, questions filling my voice.

"I have been here before," he said, gazing at the front of the building. "This was a safe inn — then."

"How long ago was that?" I asked.

"Ten, maybe fifteen years ago. Mahdi is a decent person. I will go see if there is space for us and our animals," Abram said.

I nodded, and Abram's camel knelt to the ground, allowing him to dismount. He called Danil, Bara's husband, and one of our herders, to go inside with him, then disappeared behind the heavy wooden door.

The place smelled better than most of the streets we had passed since arriving there. I sympathized with Galya. Her stomach must be churning.

Thinking of Galya, I turned, seeking her. She rode a few paces back, headscarf wrapped tightly across her face and trying not to retch.

My camel stood tied to Abram's, so I could not go to Galya, so I signaled to her to come up beside me.

"You look miserable," I said.

"Does it show?" she asked.

"Your face is green. The stench of this place must turn your stomach."

"I have fought to keep it settled since we passed through the gate."

"No doubt. The people here seem not to care about cleanliness and pleasant-smelling streets like they did in Ur or Harran."

Galya stared at our surroundings. "I wish I had a sprig of peppermint to settle my stomach."

"Perhaps the innkeeper will have some. I expected Damascus would be cleaner with all I have heard of it," I said, seeking a sign of greenery that may look like peppermint.

"I hope they have no desire to sacrifice righteous people like they did in Ur," I said, shuddering at the memory. Harran had been peaceful. The priests did not force the population to observe their sacrifices, and none of the gods they worshiped desired the blood of children.

"I wonder which gods they worshiped here in Damascus," Galya said.

"Many of the same gods worshiped in Ur and Harran, I suspect," I said.

"I saw temples to El and Mot down a side street, but Abram turned before we passed them," Yael said, riding up beside us on her brown donkey, followed by Avi.

"How sad that they do not worship Jehovah," Galya said.

"Perhaps they do not know of Jehovah," Avi said.

"Perhaps not. This is a big city with noisy, stinky people." I glanced down the street, hoping no one heard my complaint.

Bara strode forward to stand beside Yael's donkey. "Do you think we will stay here? I thought Abram would stop at one of the open fields near the gate."

"I did as well," Galya said.

"He said something about thieves," I said, gazing toward the door, willing Abram and Danil to come out.

"That makes sense," Bara said. "There were some frightening men back there."

We waited together for a time before our men finally came out a gate hidden in the wall further down.

Danil strode toward the herders and Abram waved came to join our knot of women.

"We have a place to rest," Danil called to the herders.

Abram signaled my camel to lie down and helped me dismount, then called to the other camels and took them to the front of the line of animals.

Bleating goats and sheep passed me when Abram called to them. The herders walked with them toward the gate. Horses, donkeys, and camels, the donkeys, and camels laden with our baggage, and those we rode came last. Lot followed them past the gate and out of our sight. Danil returned to stand with the women.

Only after all the animals were safely behind the walls of the inn, did Abram come for us.

"Mahdi has made room for us. It will cost us, though," he said.

I lifted my eyebrows. "I expected to pay. What does he want?"

"She wants five of our sheep. She plans to slaughter them to feed us. We can afford it." He held out his hand to me and led me toward the inn.

"She?" I asked. "I thought Mahdi was a man?"

"Mahdi is the wife of a decent man who likes his ale. She runs the inn."

"Good for her," I said. "Women should be able to run inns."

"They do here in Damascus." He took my hand and led me into the inn.

Chapter Nine

Damascus

Like every other inn we had entered since we left Ur, this one was dark, lit by a few candles. It had only one window, covered by heavy curtains to keep out the light.

"Why are inns always so dark?" I asked.

"To keep the drunks happy," a woman said from near me.

I flinched.

"I am sorry to surprise you," the tall, slender woman said. Long, dark tresses dripped from a fraying coil of hair behind her head. "Welcome to Mahdi's Inn and Tavern. I am Mahdi."

I took her extended hand and she firmly shook it.

"Abram told me a woman owned this inn. Congratulations."

"Mustafa would like to drink all our profits, but I insisted he be our guard." She turned to the side. "Mustafa!" she bellowed.

A short, burly man stepped from the shadows near her elbow. "I am here, Mahdi. You do not need to shout."

"I want to introduce you to our guests. This is Abram and his wife, Sarai."

Mustafa took my hand and bowed over it.

Abram protectively pulled me closer to him, pressing his lips into a tight grimace.

Mustafa opened his mouth in a great guffaw. "I will not touch your beautiful wife, Abram. I, like you, will defend her with my life."

"Is there a reason to protect me?" *Is this a safe inn for us to stay in?*

"We are in a city with thieves everywhere, and this is an inn with many drunken men," Mahdi said. "So, yes. You will need defence."

I shrunk into Abram's protective embrace. "Thank you," I squeaked. *Why did we stop in Damascus?*

"And these are my nephew, Lot, and his wife, Galya," Abram said, still holding me close.

"Welcome to our inn," Mustafa said. "I will protect your wife as well, Lot, as I protect Abram's. You will be safe within Mahdi's Inn and Tavern."

"Thank you," Galya said, her voice stronger than mine. "Do you have any peppermint?"

Mahdi squinted at Galya. "Sick to your stomach?"

Galya touched her stomach. "Baby."

"Ah. I will find some for you."

Mustafa laughed once more, then turned to Mahdi. "Where shall we put these guests?"

She gave him a number and he nodded. "This way, please."

"What about the rest of our people?" I asked.

"We need them to have rooms near the animals so they can protect them," Abram said. He lifted a hand. "I know you say it is safe in your paddocks, but my animals need their herders near to feel safe and to stay calm."

"There are rooms near the paddocks for your other people," Mahdi said. "They will all be safe."

"I will come down after we are settled to give you our pay," Abram said.

"Pay?" Lot questioned.

"We will give her five of our sheep to help feed all of us."

Lot nodded. "That is fair."

Mustafa led us up stone stairs and down a hall. He opened two rooms with keys and handed the keys to Abram and Lot. We entered the rooms and stared around.

I inhaled. "This is bigger than our rooms at home in Harran."

"I gave you our best rooms," Mahdi said. "You are important guests."

We walked into the sitting area with comfortable chairs and a table. We moved farther in and saw another room off to the side with a big, soft bed.

"Will our sheep be enough to pay for these rooms?" Abram asked.

"It will be more than enough," Mahdi said. "There will be enough meat for many days and many people. I will receive more than the value of these rooms."

"Do Lot and Galya have rooms as nice as this?" Abram asked.

"They do," Mustafa said. "You are all honored guests."

The couple withdrew from the room and pulled the door closed behind them. Abram pulled me into his arms and held me tight.

"I must protect you from other men."

"I am not worthy. I have not given you a child," I protested. *Would I ever feel worthy again?*

"A child will come," Abram whispered. "Be patient. I am."

I sighed and leaned into his muscular chest and his love. *How long would he love me? How long would his patience last? For now, I would depend on his love.*

Lot knocked and he and Galya entered our rooms. "We wanted to see if your rooms are as nice as ours." They paused in the center of the sitting area, gazing at our rooms. "Yours are nicer."

"But not by much," Galya said. "How did we get such elegant rooms?"

"I do not know. It must be our willingness to pay in sheep," Abram said.

"Your reputation proceeds you all the way to Damascus," Lot said. "Mahdi will have many more guests when others learn you honored her with your visit."

Abram shrugged. "You need to rest, Sarai. It has been a difficult journey. We will stay here a few days."

"We should leave sooner than a few days," I said. "I could get too comfortable in these spacious rooms and not want to return to my tent."

"So true, Sarai," Galya said. "Are you certain Damascus is not the place Jehovah wants us to settle?"

"This is nice," Lot said.

Abram grinned. "Perhaps. But we could not stay in these rooms if we do. I will ask Jehovah."

I knew he had already spoken to Jehovah about where we were to go. He had promised us a land of our own. Damascus was not our home.

Abram settled me on a comfortable chair, kissed me, and ordered me to rest. He and Lot then left to decide which of the sheep to give to Mahdi as payment.

Galya stayed with me to keep me company. Mahdi brought in a tray of sweet, juicy fruits to quench our thirst and hunger as we waited for the mutton to be prepared.

"This is a lovely place," Galya said. "I would love to stay here."

"We could not afford to give away our animals to stay here," I said. "Damascus is a big city. I do not feel comfortable in big cities anymore."

"The gods do not demand human sacrifice here," Galya said.

"Not that we know of. I do not want to have them change their minds and expect their priests to sacrifice Abram or me."

"This is a comfortable place to rest while you recover."

"For today, maybe tomorrow. But I know there is a land for us farther on."

"You would not want to travel onward tomorrow?" Galya said with a gasp. "Not so soon."

"No. We will want to go to the market to replenish our supplies before we leave. But we cannot stay long. I fear these people."

I did not know why, but Damascus brought chills of fear, not the excitement it promised, and I wanted to leave as soon as we could.

"These people?" Galya searched the room for others. "What people? There is no one here to fear. Certainly not Mahdi nor Mustafa?"

"No. I do not fear Mahdi or Mustafa. It is the others here. I sense danger."

Galya shook her head and laughed. "We are safe here."

"Yes, here within the walls of Mahdi's Inn, we are safe. I do not believe we are safe anywhere else in this city."

"The city guards will protect us," Galya insisted.

"How many city guards did you see as we made our way through the city streets to this inn?"

Galya stopped giggling and glared at me. "None, after we came through the gate."

"Exactly. None. Which of those 'none' guards do you expect to protect you?"

"Lot and Abram."

"They and our herders are the only protection we will have, except maybe Mustafa, while we are within the walls of Mahdi's inn."

Swallowing my fears, I went to the market with Galya and some of the other women the next day. Mustafa refused to allow us only our husbands and a few others for protection. He led the way, turning on roads that caused Abram's eyebrows to rise. He and the other men kept their hands on their swords, prepared for attack.

We reached the market and purchased our supplies with no problems. However, as we trooped away, a disturbance made us hurry. Loud voices increased my tension. Men were fighting near the exit. Abram, Lot, and the other men surrounded us and hurried us away.

Once more, Mustafa led the way, taking side streets, rather than the main roads that would take us directly to the inn. The noise died away as we moved farther from the market.

At last, we reached the inn and Mustafa ushered us all into the tavern and seated us at tables. "You are lucky to all arrive safely. They meant that fight as a diversion, to draw your men into the fight so they could take your women."

"Why would they want us?" Avi asked, her eyes wide.

"Slaves," Bara said. "Is that not so, Master Mustafa?"

Mustafa ducked his head. "Yes. The Ziaeddin targeted your women."

"Who are the Ziaeddin?" Galya asked.

Abram and Lot focused their glare on Mustafa.

He swallowed. "Thieves and robbers who hide in the shadows. They take women for slaves ... and..." Mustafa gulped. "They do things that should not happen to women."

"We were blessed to have Mustafa with us today," Abram said.

I narrowed my eyes at Mustafa. "How do you know the Ziaeddin are targeting us?"

He gazed back at me. "I have a spy in their ranks, so I can protect Mahdi and our guests. He warned me that the Ziaeddin were seeking women."

Galya gasped. "Will we be safe here?"

"Inside the walls of Mahdi's Inn you are safe. Outside, not so much," Mustafa said.

We stayed in the inn for three days, celebrating the Sabbath in the space near the animal paddocks. Abram and the other men purchased the last of the supplies we would need to travel south toward Canaan, where Jehovah had sent us.

Early in the morning of the fourth day, we mounted our camels and quietly passed through the gates of Mahdi's Inn and Tavern. Mustafa and Abram led us through the streets toward the nearest gate.

Some of Mustafa's men joined us, surrounding the women and animals. All our men had swords out, watching into the darkness for the men who would twist a name meaning splendor of religion into something evil.

I shrunk into my saddle. We had dressed our heads to look like men, tucking our hair into the turbans men of Damascus wore. I stared into the dark shadows, seeing enemies in everyone, expecting them to see through our deception. We rode in silence. Even the sheep and goats did not bleat.

Mustafa led us along streets I had never seen, turning often to confuse any who may have laid traps for us. The stars were dimming when we finally approached a city gate. He rode ahead and spoke in low tones to the guards. Something passed between their hands before the gate swung open and we ambled past them.

Mustafa and his men stayed with us for the next two days. We stopped at a spring the night of the second day.

"I believe we are far enough away from Damascus now," Mustafa said. "My men and I will leave you in the morning. The Ziaeddin will not come this far into the wilderness to steal women."

We settled into our beds that night, finally believing we were safe. But in the darkest part of the night, men shouted.

"Stay here!" Abram cried as he leapt from our bed, grabbed his sword, and rushed from our tent.

I crouched in our tent as I listened to the cries and shouts of men and the clashing of swords. Our men would require healing. The noise of the battle came close to our tent, then ebbed away for a time, before coming close once more.

I shuddered as I found my belt knife and held it ready. No Ziaeddin would take me as their prisoner.

The noise of the battle dimmed. At last, Abram staggered into our tent. "They are gone, those who live."

I gasped. "And our men? Did we lose any?"

"None are dead, but some are injured." He cradled his arm against his body.

"And you? How badly did they hurt your arm?"

"Not much," Abram said.

I lit a lamp and took his arm. An enemy had slashed it. When I washed it, however, I discovered the injury did not cut deeply.

I wrapped it with a clean cloth and gathered my healing mixtures and bandages and nodded toward the tent opening. "We must see to the other injured men."

Abram sighed, took a lamp, and led the way into the night. The other women had tended to our men's injuries. However, some of Mustafa's men and some attackers lay moaning in the dirt.

I bent to help the nearest man. He grabbed my skirts. "Help me," he pled.

Abram bent to pull him away, but I had already gently disentangled his fingers from my hem. "Where are you injured?"

The man moaned as I touched him, searching for the injury.

"Here," Abram said, pulling back the tunic from his body.

A sword had sliced into him, cutting him open. I could do little for such a serious wound. Still, Abram helped me bind it together. As I gently tied it together, hoping not to cause greater pain, he breathed his last breath.

"May your God bless you for the care you gave my servant," Mustafa said from the edge of the circle of onlookers.

"He did not live," I said.

"But he died in the care of a gentle and beautiful woman. His mother and wife will find peace in that."

A tear slid down my cheek. "I grieve for his wife. Are there more injured?"

Mustafa shook his head. "Only this man who did not survive. All the others had cuts they could care for. Those of the Ziaeddin who did not run away will no longer hurt others." He brushed his hands together.

"What did you do?" Abram asked.

"I sent them to their gods. They should not have attacked our camp."

I glanced up, seeing the graying light of morning. "Will we need to fear that others will attack us?"

"I doubt it. We will bury their dead and leave markers for them to find if they choose to return for the bodies." Abram brushed the dirt from his robes. "Then, we move onward."

"I will take this one with my other men home to his wife," Mustafa said, bowing over the body of his dead servant. "You will be safe from the Ziaeddin. Mahdi will need my protection."

"Travel safely, my friend," Abram said.

Mustafa somberly wrapped the body of his servant and tied him across his donkey. He and his men mounted their animals and rode away into the rising sun.

During the morning meal, I saw many with bandaged arms and legs, but none of our men had injuries needing further care. Jehovah had blessed us.

We packed our possessions onto our camels and left the little spring behind, once more safe and protected by Jehovah.

Chapter Ten

Drought

After traveling many days on the well-worn road used by traders and thieves, Abram told us we would soon arrive in Jerash. I expected to see another walled city like Ur or Damascus. When we did not see tall walls in the distance, I hoped to see the mud and wooden walls like Harran had.

But Jerash was not as big as Harran. A few mud huts circled a well but did not even have walls to protect their women.

Abram entered the small village with Lot to request the use of the well for our animals. We set up our tents a distance from their tiny village, then Abram, Lot, and our herders led the animals to the well where they gave them water.

When the men returned, they slaughtered two sheep which we cooked over our fires. We shared them with the people of Jerash.

"It is only right that we help feed these people," Abram said.

"Their village looks poor," I said.

"And they will share their water with us, even in their poverty."

"Is there anything else we can do for them?"

"Perhaps."

The next morning, I watched Abram build an altar and offer sacrifice to Jehovah. As he prayed, I echoed his prayers in my mind. We begged Him to relieve the drought that continued to plague Ur, Harran, and Damascus.

"What is this place called?" I asked Abram.

"Jershon. Jehovah promised us a place of inheritance."

"Is this where we are to stay?"

"Not here. This is not to be our land of inheritance."

"This place is dry."

"I see little water flowing into the well, too. We would become a vexing situation for these villagers."

"We have many animals and people and not enough water. We must continue onward, much as I would love to stay here."

Abram agreed. We left the remnants of the mutton we cooked with the people of Jerash and moved farther south, seeking the home Jehovah had promised us.

We traveled onward through a dead and dying earth, for the drought had spread to this place as well. I could not even find the tiny flowers that brightened my hope before we arrived in Damascus.

We passed into the territory of Canaan, hoping to find people who believed in Jehovah. Our shoulders drooped when we learned that the people here served idols.

What entices people to worship idols?

Jehovah had allowed the drought to fill this place as he had the others we had passed through.

We came to a plain called Moreh, or fruitful, by those who lived near there. There in Sichem, Abram offered sacrifice to Jehovah, begging for the drought to end and bless this country and the others we had passed. He begged for his father to survive the drought in Harran.

He left the caravan for a time after the sacrifice as he often did to commune with Jehovah. I contemplated the sacrifice and our travel, tired of traveling, hoping Jehovah would tell Abram to rest here. Although drought continued to afflict this land, a small stream ran through the plain and I could hope for a home. I would love a place where we could stay, a place where the animals could go to pasture in the morning and return home at night. That would be heaven, even if the home was a tent.

When Abram returned late that night, I waited at the door of our tent. He gave me the good news. Although he slumped from exhaustion, his face seemed to shine. "We are to settle here for a time. This is the edge of the home Jehovah has given to us and our posterity. Sichem."

Joy filled me. Home at last. "The edge?" I asked. *Edge, a sliver, all? I did not care, as long as we could settle here for a time.*

"Yes, for we are to inherit all of Canaan. This is but the shoulder, a part of the whole."

"Are we allowed to stay here?"

"For a time. We move our animals and tents tomorrow, then we will stay for a time in this beautiful country Jehovah has given to us. This will be our home."

I peered about the darkened countryside, seeing what had been tall grass and flowers, now bent to the ground, drying and lifeless. "It would be beautiful with rain."

"Jehovah will cause the drought to end when the people remember Him."

Abram's confidence caused me to smile.

He thrust his chest out. "You doubt me?"

"I do not doubt you. I doubt these people who have faith in their idol gods will ever remember the one true God."

"Jehovah is patient. They will return to him, one day."

"In our lifetime?" I scrunched my eyes closed. "I do not see that happening."

"Enough Jehovah will forgive them and cause this desert to bloom."

"I could live with blooms, but does another claim this area?"

"If he does, we will purchase it from him. This shall be our home."

Early the next morning, we traveled again, as we had for the past months. But this time, we left the traveled road and moved west, toward the great sea. The camels climbed up a small hill and Abram brought them to a halt.

"This is where we are to live," he said at last. "Water flows beneath us. The grass is green and sweet for the animals. This will be our home."

Soon, men had tents pitched in a small circle. The men built fences to mark the animals' paddock. The herders left with the sheep and goats, taking them to green pastures farther up the hill.

I opened my baskets and removed dishes and other home goods I had not taken out while we traveled. We were home. Unexpected tension released within me. I set out pillows and dishes, my nicest lamps and my best blankets.

Abram opened our travel table and chairs, setting them in the front of the tent. Behind a flap, he set up our bed. I set out the lamps, pillows, blankets, and dishes. Abram found other small tables, setting them along the edge of the tent. On these, I set trays and other beautiful things to show we were home.

Abram sat in a chair in the doorway and sighed. "We are home again."

"Even a tent can be a home," I said, reclining back, enjoying the view of my new domain. Home. I shivered in delight.

"It can."

I leaned back and closed my eyes. "It is good to be settled for a time."

Abram leaned across the space between our chairs and kissed me. "Perhaps being settled will help us have children."

"It could," I said. *It has never helped before.*

Abram stood and lifted me from my chair.

"Where are we going?" I asked, slapping his shoulder playfully.

"To create a child."

I giggled as he carried me to our bed. Inside, I prayed to Jehovah, begging him to give us a child this time.

No child came at that time. Jehovah's promises to Abram continued to be held in reserve. Would I ever give him the child promised to him? Would I ever become a mother?

Not now. I mourned each month as my womanly bleeding laid me low. When, Jehovah? When will my womb no longer be barren? When will I carry a child?

Even at nearly seventy, I hoped for a child. Eve had given birth long after her hundredth year.

"Nothing is impossible with Jehovah," Abram reminded me. "You will have a child."

The grass drooped in the heat. We searched daily toward the west, hoping for rain to blow in from the great sea. A few fluffy white clouds floated high over our heads toward the east, but none darkened and filled with enough water to drop it on us.

The stream that flowed through our valley became smaller as it dried. Our animals struggled to find enough food and water to stay alive.

One afternoon, Lot hurried to our tent. "It is Galya's time. Bara is with her now. What do I do?"

"Join us as we wait," Abram said. "It is what men do."

We could hear Galya's moans and cries in the distance.

"I should go to her, but I have never given birth," I said, wringing my hands.

"Bara is with her," Abram said.

"And her daughter, who knows about giving birth," Lot added.

We listened to Galya well into the night. When at last we heard a tiny cry, we knew her child had come into the world. I swallowed my pain and smiled and gave Lot an embrace. After a time, when the child and Galya were cleaned and ready, Bara invited us in to meet Galya's little girl.

Lot lifted his tiny daughter into his arms. I watched, wrapped in Abram's protective arms. We cooed at her beauty and left.

Later, Abram held me close in our bed, consoling me in my anguish. My sobs of self-pity slowly diminished in Abram's love and promise that I would have a child one day.

Lot and Galya named their daughter Rona, meaning joy. She brought them much joy.

We watched for cool weather to arrive, hoping it would also bring moisture with it. Food had become scarce. We could no longer trade our wool for needed grains with those who lived in the surrounding region. They had no food to share. Their children began to suffer from lack of food and water. I feared we would soon endure a similar loss.

And when the season changed and cool weather came, the rain stayed away. Some rain fell on the mountain above us, bringing some water back to our stream, but not enough for all our animals.

We traveled to Sichem once more so Abram could offer another sacrifice and beg Jehovah for a break in the drought so we could grow the necessary food once more.

He shared the news with us after communing with Jehovah. "We must leave this place. Jehovah has commanded that we continue on to Egypt. The drought is not affecting them there as it is here in the north."

My heart lurched in my chest. If Ur was a wicked city, surely the cities of Egypt would be worse. Elkanah, whose priests wanted to sacrifice Abram, was a god of the pharaohs of Egypt. It sickened me to think of Abram tied to the altar.

"What about Elkanah?" I asked.

"Jehovah will protect us. We are going there because He commanded it, not because we choose to leave this dry region."

"It was not always this dry. I can see it was once a beautiful country."

"But the drought has changed it. We can no longer get enough food for everyone. We must go."

We left Sichem to return to the hills with heavy hearts, returning to our tent home to pack our possessions once more to be placed on the backs of camels and donkeys. I almost felt betrayed to leave this country, our promised home. But if we were to live, we must go. Our herders and their wives and families were soon ready to depart, as were Abram and I.

We were to ride south once more, seeking water and a safe place to live. I did not savor the coming aching back and sore legs that came from riding many miles. However, Jehovah had commanded it. And the stream had dried to a narrow trickle. We had no choice about it. We had to move on.

I gazed around the valley that had become our home, memorizing the notch in the hills, the stream bed that once flowed with water, and the fields that were once covered with flowers. Abram had promised we would return some day.

Early the next morning, we rose in the dark, loaded our possessions, and mounted as the dark became milky before dawn.

The sky to the east lightened and became pink and gold as the sun rose. In its beauty, I believed we would find a place to live with sufficient water for us and all our animals.

Days later, I searched the distance, hoping the walls of Egypt would appear.

In my early days, my father had taught me to always look for the small beauties in my life, proof of Jehovah's love. To avoid boredom and the monotony of riding, I searched for splendor. I saw tiny blue star flowers growing beside the path. There were patterns blown in the sand. I marveled at fluffy clouds in a brilliant blue sky and hoped they would darken and bring us water. My eyes followed birds of many colors clinging to dry branches, feeding off the dried seeds from seasons before, and wondered why the wind had not blown them away earlier. These things and multiple other things caught my eyes and filled my soul with wonder and gratitude to Jehovah for the beauties of the earth.

Abram noticed my improved attitude and commented on it.

"I watch for little evidences of beauty. Even here in this dry place, Jehovah sends his beauty."

"Little things?" Abram mused. "Like what?"

I pointed at a tiny yellow star-shaped flower growing close to the ground. "Like that. How does such a beautiful flower grow in this desert wilderness?"

Abram stared at the ground as his camel passed the little bed of flowers. "How did I not see these?"

"Or that?" I said, pointing to a wolf in the distance.

"The wolf? I thought he would frighten you." Surprise filled his voice.

"He is a gift. He, too, seeks food and water. He would not be here if water did not flow somewhere close."

"That makes sense. I had not thought to look for beauty in the world as we travel. I worry about robbers and where we will next stop to rest for the night." Abram waved at the shadows surrounding us.

"Father taught me to seek the beauty everywhere."

"I have heard you speak of this before. I will try to remember to seek beauty, not just watch the shadows for danger."

"You are welcome to watch the shadows for danger. If you did not, I could not seek beauty."

"Point some out to me so I can enjoy them, too," he said.

I grinned. "I would be happy to do that."

As we rode, we made a game of finding beauty. Even Lot and Galya joined us, as did the herders and their wives. Soon our search for hidden beauty broke the tedium of travel. Women giggled and called to each other to see new and amazing beauties. From then until we finally saw the walls of Memphis, the city of the pharaohs, we seldom found ourselves filled with boredom.

Galya rode with her babe strapped in a pack close to her chest. When little Rona needed food or changing, her mother loosened the straps and took care of her needs. It helped that we rode in cushioned comfort, on wide platforms and pavilions shielding us from the sun. Rona could sleep near her mother without fear of falling.

We camped for the last night less than a day's ride away from the walls of Memphis.

As we prepared for bed that evening, Abram was unusually quiet.

"What is going on in that beautiful head of yours?" I asked, running my fingers through his thick, curly, dark hair.

"Thinking," he murmured.

"Of what?" I massaged his head.

"Of the instructions Jehovah gave me in the night."

"Oh?" My hands hesitated, then continued to move across his head and shoulders.

"Pharaoh is an important man. You are a beautiful woman."

"Me, beautiful? I am in my sixties," I scoffed.

"And still a beautiful woman." He caught my hand and brought it to his lips to kiss it.

"What has that to do with us? What has it to do with the message Jehovah gave you?"

"Pharaoh will want you for his wife."

I felt light-headed and tightened my hands into fists in his hair. I wanted no part of that. "I hear Pharaoh already has many wives. Why would he want me?" I moved in front of Abram, knelt at his feet, and stared into his face.

Tears streaked across his cheeks as he rubbed his chest.

"It is his way. If he knows I am married to you, he will kill me to have you. Jehovah commands us to tell Pharaoh you are my sister, not my wife. It will save my life."

I reeled in shock. A coldness filled me to the center of my being. "But I am your wife. We covenanted with Jehovah."

"And Pharaoh will kill me to get you."

"Is there no other way?"

Abram's mournful eyes told me there was no other solution.

"I am yours. No other man can have me. I will not go into the city. We can live along the river." Tears formed in the corners of my eyes and dripped onto my chest as I searched his face for reassurance.

"I am commanded to go to Pharaoh. I have knowledge he needs." Abram touched my cheek with the back of his hand. "Help me with this. You do not want him to kill me. We can find a way out of this. Jehovah will protect you. That is part of our covenant."

Tears streamed down my face. "If I lie, if I say you are my brother, he will not kill you?" I hoped he would smile and tell me he had misunderstood. But he did not.

"That is what Jehovah has warned. If you say you are my sister, Jehovah will protect you ... and me." Abram pulled me into his arms.

I leaned into his arms, wanting to be closer than I had ever been. After we entered Memphis, would my kind, gentle, sweet husband ever hold me again? Would Pharaoh take me as his wife? I fought to breathe. No. I could not leave my beloved for another man. How? Disgust sickened me.

But I could not cause his death. Jehovah had promised Abram many children and, because of me, he still had none.

I turned from his kisses. "Why would Jehovah send us to Egypt if we must pretend this way?"

My tears now mingled with his as we held each other close.

A voice, a thought, filled my mind. *Agree to this. I will save your lives and your honor. Do not fear. Trust me.*

Jehovah! Could I trust Him? How could I not trust him?

"You are my husband," I sobbed, "and I will do as you say. I will not like it. I desire to be near you, always."

"I pray Pharaoh will take us into his home, so I can be near you. This cannot last long. Jehovah sent us so I could teach Pharaoh."

I leaned back on my knees and wiped at my tears. "What will you teach him?"

"About the stars and alignments, and other things Jehovah has taught me. Perhaps even of Jehovah. I am no mere shepherd. I have much knowledge."

"Will Pharaoh know that?" I asked.

"I will wear my best robes and ask to be taken to him when we enter the city. Stay near me, as you always do, but do not be surprised if I say you are my sister."

My stomach churned, but I trusted Jehovah. "I do not want to be only your sister. I am your wife." I gazed into his eyes, filled with sorrow and pain. He did not like this any more than I did. "But I will do as you and Jehovah command. I will claim I am your sister."

Abram pulled me onto his lap and kissed me. How long would I be required to avoid his arms? How long before I could be his wife once more?

All that night, we held each other close.

Chapter Eleven

Abram's Sister

The towering white stone walls of Memphis glistened in the early afternoon sunlight. I had never seen stones glitter as these did. I wondered what stones would cause it to glitter as it did. Their brightness forced us to pull our headscarves across our faces to avoid the blinding light.

The gates gaped open with guards standing in the shadows. They stepped forward.

"Who are you? What is your business here?" one demanded.

"I am Abram, a prince of Ur. I come to speak to the mighty Pharaoh."

Prince of Ur? I suppose there is some truth in that, but few princes escape after the priests try to sacrifice them.

The guards frowned at our caravan and all the animals bunching together, waiting for permission to enter the vast city of Memphis.

"And what gifts do you bring to Pharaoh?" another guard demanded.

"I have knowledge for him."

"Pharaoh is great. He has all knowledge."

"Not this knowledge," Abram insisted. "I also have a colt, son of the finest horse in all Ur and Canaan."

The guards looked down their long noses at us, then gestured to a younger man. "Lead this 'Prince of Ur' to Pharaoh."

The young man bowed. "This way, Prince."

We followed him through the busy streets. A boy scampered past, with a guard behind us shouting, "Hurry! You must arrive before the caravan."

"Messenger telling Pharaoh of our coming," Abram murmured.

I nodded.

The young man who guided us turned, leading us along a wide road bordering on the river. Bricks up past the camel's knees bordered the river.

"What do you call the river?" I asked.

"We call it the Black," our guide said. "Many outsiders call it the Nile, but it has been the Black since we settled here."

I nodded and quietly rode beside Abram along the river. The slowly moving water cooled us from the heat of the summer.

Our guide stopped and pointed to troughs near the river. "Your herders can give your animals water."

"How will we get the water from the river to the water troughs?" Lot asked.

Our guide showed him how the shaduf worked. He dropped the bucket into the canal, then guided it to the troughs, where Danil and the other herders dumped the water into the trough. Danil directed a herder to take over managing the shaduf.

"This is an interesting system for getting water from the river," Abram said.

"It is an invention of an early Pharaoh. We have used it for many years."

"It works well," Lot said.

We sat on our camels' backs while they dipped their massive noses into the water and slurped it up. When they had their fill, herders brought up the horses, donkeys, sheep, goats, and dogs to drink. It took an hour for all the animals to drink.

When the last lamb stepped away from the water, our guide lifted a gate and the water sluiced back into the river.

The boy who had run past us as we entered the city ran up to our guide and whispered in his ear.

"The Pharaoh awaits you," our guide said. "We must hurry. This way."

He led us away from the river inland until we reached towering walls surrounding buildings. "This is Pharaoh's home," our guide said. He turned to the men at the gates. "Pharaoh is expecting this Prince of Ur."

A guard nodded. "Come with me, Prince of Ur. Bring your people. The animals can follow Makt." He gestured to a nearby man dressed in a short kilt.

"You herders, go with Makt. Settle the animals. And Danil?" Abram said, ordering his camel to kneel. Mine knelt beside it.

"Yes, master?" Danil said.

Abram slid off. "Brush and curry the colt so he shines when I present him to the Pharaoh."

Danil bowed his head.

Abram helped me off my camel while Lot and Galya dismounted theirs. Galya lifted her little Rona into her arms.

Our guard led the way and I walked with Abram. Lot and Galya followed. There was no need to imply that Galya was Lot's sister with their young daughter.

We walked up many low stairs to reach the door to Pharaoh's home. A guard opened the door and nodded to the guard with us.

Inside, another servant, dressed in a kilt a little longer than the one worn by Makt, led us into the building, down a long passageway, to another door. There, guards stood with lances crossed in front of it.

"I bring the Prince of Ur and his friends," our guard said.

A man who guarded the door stepped forward. "You may not carry any weapons into the presence of our glorious Pharaoh."

Abram and Lot removed their swords and set them in an urn beside the guard.

"Your swords will be safe here. You may retrieve them when you leave."

"Thank you," Abram murmured.

Our men looked elegant in the dress robes they had donned that morning, especially compared to the Egyptian men dressed in short kilts. Galya and I had dressed in our finest dresses and layered light shawls over them, with airy headscarves covering our hair.

A guard opened the door and spoke with a man inside. He nodded to us and gestured for us to follow him into an enormous room.

Inside the room, I gazed in awe at the walls lined with sheer fabric covering murals depicting marvelous deeds of previous pharaohs. I glanced up at the ceiling, much higher than even inside the temples of Ur.

This place, grander than any I had entered in Ur, overwhelmed me. Would Pharaoh ask me to live here? Would I want to live in such luxury? Not without Abram.

Off to one side, a fountain bubbled with water spilling into a basin. The coolness of the room refreshed me after riding through the scorching sun.

We walked past men and women gathered in the room. These men wore long kilts of fine linen, some sweeping past their knees. The women wore colorful linen dresses, most brushing the floor. When I glanced at their bodies, however, I had to mask my surprise with a small cough. Many of the dresses rose only to the bottom of their bosoms, leaving them uncovered. A few covered their nipples. Fewer still had dresses covering their bosoms. I shuddered at the sight.

I looked into their faces. They watched us pass with detachment. Their semi-nakedness appeared natural to them. What would this Pharaoh think of me covered in more than one layer?

Worse, what would I do if Pharaoh expects me to dress like these women and show my body as they did? Bile filled my throat at the thought. I would need to stand up for myself. Perhaps my modesty would prevent him desiring me.

The men and women stepped back as our guide led us forward. I did not want to look at a man who would take me as his wife. He had one. More than one if rumors were true. He did not need me.

Abram nudged me. "We should bow," he murmured.

I bowed, keeping my eyes on the floor. I wanted to reach out to take Abram's hand, but I remembered. Here I was his sister, not his wife. As the hair on the back of my neck rose in warning, I kept my hands at my side.

Someone approached us, but I did not look up. Feet stepped close, circling me. Pharaoh. With clammy hands and a racing heart, I inhaled silently and waited. If I did not look at him, maybe he would not want me. Why would he want an old woman? *Jehovah protect me. You promised me safety.* My heart pounded less noisily.

A leather-wrapped stick settled against my chin. "Look at me."

I flicked a quick peek at Abram who nodded before I lifted my head.

"You are?" the man said.

I stared ahead, not wanting to look at him. "Sarai."

"Why did the messenger not tell me a beautiful woman accompanied the Prince of Ur?"

"Perhaps he did not know, Lord Pharaoh," Abram said. "He left the guardhouse so quickly. I doubt he had time to assess the beauty of our women."

The men and women in the room tittered.

Pharaoh walked around me three more times, while I refused to look at him. "Look at me," he whispered.

At last, I looked up into the face of a handsome man with dark brown hair curling down to his shoulders and a pleasant smile on his face. His bearing commanded respect. I could see he knew he held all the power in the room.

I swallowed thickly, praying I did not say or do something wrong that would betray Abram. I could not live if he did not.

"Is this Prince of Ur your husband?" he asked.

"No, Pharaoh. Abram is my ..." I swallowed, "my brother."

"Your sister?" He looked at Abram.

He nodded. "She is my sister."

I fought back the tears that struggled to flow across my cheeks, forcing them to flow inside rather than out where Pharaoh could see them.

"Good. I would not want to kill you in order to take this beautiful woman as my wife." He tipped his head back and chortled.

The men and women of the court politely laughed with him.

He would kill my Abram if he knew. He still could if he finds out. I had not believed he would. *Forgive my unbelief, Jehovah.*

"I want you to be my wife," Pharaoh said. "You do not mind, do you, Prince of Ur?"

"My name is Abram," Abram said in an even voice, refusing to betray our grief. "I do not mind. She is my sister."

I glanced toward him, hoping for a final longing glance. It did not come.

Pharaoh turned and clapped his hands. Women from somewhere along the edge of the room rushed forward to hurry me away before I could say anything. I had no choice.

I turned my head to look at Abram over my shoulder. His eyes followed me with his lips pressed tightly together, unable to say or do anything.

"Come, sit with me, Abram. My messenger said you have a gift for me?"

"Yes, I brought you a colt, one of the finest I have ever seen."

The women ushered me from the room and down another passage, making turns until I no longer knew where I was. My shoulders were tighter than I had ever felt them. I wanted to race away from it all, to stop and never move again, to scream my agony in piercing cries. But I did not. I timidly followed the women.

I longed to see Abram again. And we had only been separated for a few moments. Why would Jehovah bring us here, where I must pretend to be his sister, not his wife? I feared Pharaoh would force me to break the sacred vows we made on our marriage day. *Jehovah, forbid!*

The women led me into a part of the building they called the women's quarters. Two took my hands and led me into a room with a deep pool of water.

"Come with me," a pretty young woman dressed in a shorter dress than the women in the audience room wore.

"Who are you?" I asked.

"I am Ami," the tall girl said.

"And I am Sanura," the girl on the other side of me said.

Both girls giggled. Both were tall, lithe, young women with straight dark hair and golden-brown skin.

"What will you do with me?" I asked.

"Pharaoh likes his women washed and perfumed before he meets them in the women's' quarters."

I gulped. "Meets his women? How many wives does he have?"

The girls giggled again. "He has many women," Sanura said. "I do not know how many wives he has."

"We are among his women, though. Daughters of his wives," Ami added. "You will join us."

Their hands reached for my clothing.

"I can take my clothing off myself," I said, holding my hands against the shoulders of my dress.

"Yafeu assigned us to help you. Would you have us chastised for not doing as ordered?" Ami asked, no longer giggling.

I thought about her words. *I do not want to be the cause of another's punishment.* I moved my hands. "No. I do not want you chastised."

Ami and Sanura gently removed the scarf from my head and the light shawl from my shoulders.

"Does he ... take his new women right away?"

Ami giggled. "He will come to you and sit and talk, but he will not bed you right away."

I sighed. *Jehovah, keep him from my bed.*

They folded my clothes and set them on a bench.

"This is beautiful," Ami said. "What is it made of?"

"Wool from our sheep and goats," I said. "I wove it."

"You wove this? You a princess of Ur?"

"I did. I weave fabrics to give me something to do."

"Is it difficult?" Sanura asked.

"Not for me. I have woven fabrics since I was a little girl."

Ami's eyes widened. "You did not have slaves or servants to do these things?"

"My family had servants, but my mother believed I should learn to work. She taught me to weave."

Sanura and Ami lifted my dress over my head. Sanura fingered the design on the hem of my dress. "Surely a servant stitched this design?"

"No. I did that. I made my dress as well."

"Why, if you have servants?" Ami asked, unbinding my hair.

"What else am I to do with my time all day?"

Sanura crunched her eyebrows close together. "We bathe, sing, and play games."

They led me into the pool. I shivered in the cool water, but sank below its surface, allowing my hair to get wet.

"You must get your water from the river to have so much available for bathing," I said.

Ami widened her eyes and gave a little shrug. "I do not know where we get this water. It is here. Is that not enough?" She took my arm and washed it while Sanura washed the other.

I shook my head. *Young women who did not question. What have they done to them?* "Have you ever lived outside these women's quarters?"

The young women gasped. "No! Our mothers birthed us in the birthing room over there," Ami said, nodding off toward another part of the women's area. "We have never left the walls of Pharaoh's palace."

"You call him Pharaoh. Is he not your father?"

Sanura's tinkling laugh filled the room. She filled her hands with soap. "Perhaps. Duck beneath the water once more and we will wash your hair."

I did as they asked, coming up from the water splashing them. We all giggled. It was good to play with these young women. It helped to calm my nerves.

"We do not know who our father is," Ami said as she helped to wash my hair. "It is enough that we live here in Pharaoh's household."

"And bathe, and eat, and sleep, and play music, and play," I murmured.

"Yes. It is a satisfying life," Sanura said.

Is it? Can I live this way after being the mistress of my own home, after loving and being loved by Abram? What will I do if Pharaoh chooses me?

After Ami and Sanura led me from the pool, they dried and dressed my body and hair with sweet smelling perfumes. They put a dress like theirs on me, light linen pleated from the neckline. Sanura tried to pull it below my bosoms, but I pulled it up.

"But it is our way," Ami protested.

"It is not my way. I am from Ur and Canaan. I do not display my body in such a way." *My bosoms are for Abram.*

They gave up and brushed my hair and dressed it in long loops. They pinned it up with jeweled combs.

Sanura led me to a tall oval of polished copper. "See. You are beautiful, fit to be seen with Pharaoh."

I gazed into the reflection. I was beautiful. Dressed and washed like this, I hardly recognized myself as an old woman. My skin did not wrinkle as many at my age, and my hair still shone. But I still wanted to be with Abram.

"Where now?" I asked.

"Our steward, Yafeu, will assign you a sleeping space. Then we will introduce you to the other women."

As they led me away, I questioned what would happen next. *Where was Abram? When could I see him again?*

Chapter Twelve

Hagar

After Yafeu showed me my rooms and gave me instructions, Ami and Sanura introduced me to the women. Many smiled through their teeth, but few truly welcomed me. They greeted me, then returned to their gossiping.

I leaned back on a seat away from the gossiping women, thinking of Abram. *What was he doing? Did Pharaoh accept the gift of the colt?*

A colt. A wife. He got a bargain when Abram came to Memphis.

An older woman slipped into the seat beside mine. "I am Nabukha."

"I am Sarai."

Her smile was genuine and warm. "I remember from when Ami introduced us. I did not think you would remember my name, with so many to remember."

"You remember all the names of these women?" I asked.

"I have been here many years. I was one of the first women he took before he married Senet."

"Senet? Which one is that?"

Nabukha's eyes darted about the room. "She does not always grace us with her presence, but she is there," she tilted her head toward the knot of gossiping women. "In the middle of the rumor mongering women. You present a problem for them."

"Me? A problem? How?"

"You are new competition, and you are lovely, even though you are older than most women Pharaoh brings to his women's quarters."

"Competition? I did not desire to be here." I fought to keep the whine from my voice. *Competition for Pharaoh? Did they not know I wanted nothing to do with him? I only wanted to be reunited with Abram.*

"Yet you are, and the others fear you will take what little power they have from them."

"Power? I want none of that. I want to leave when my brother leaves. I do not desire to be one of Pharaoh's women."

"That sets you apart." Nabukha tossed her head toward the knot of conniving women. "You know who you are and do not choose to be here. You have an elegance they can never have."

We sat together, softly visiting. Nabukha shared with me the unspoken rules of the women's quarters.

Eventually, servants brought huge trays of food, fresh fruits, savory meats, roasted vegetables, warm flat bread, and wine. Nabukha and I ate together.

As I waited for Pharaoh to come to the women's quarters, I became jittery inside. *Would he want to take me to bed tonight? Where was Abram? I missed him.*

Followed by only one guard, Pharaoh entered much later than I expected. The sun had set and the lamps lit. I had hoped he would not come.

But he came, loudly laughing and calling to the women, searching for me. I did not hide, but I did not stand up to be found.

"There you are," he called when he finally caught sight of me and Nabukha sitting together, away from the other women. "I had begun to wonder if you got lost here in my women's quarters."

I stood and bowed to him.

Nabukha pulled on my skirts and hissed, "We do not bow in here."

I straightened my back.

Pharaoh's booming laugh filled the room. "Abram tells me you are handy. He says you wove a tapestry showing the placement of the stars."

"I did. Abram tells me it is an accurate depiction."

"I would like to see it." His voice lowered as he came to sit in the seat Nabukha vacated. "Sit."

I reclaimed my seat. "It is with my other things in my baggage. I do not know where they are."

"Abram said the same thing. I have ordered your baggage taken to your room."

My face lit up. "I am to have my things? May I wear my own clothing as well?"

"Stand. Let me look at you," he ordered.

Confused, I resumed my upright position in front of him.

"Turn." He waggled his finger in a circle.

I spun.

"Slowly," he said with a little laugh.

I turned slowly so he could see me.

"You look lovely in our clothing, but I see no reason you could not wear yours sometimes."

I bowed my head. "Thank you."

"Sit and talk with me."

I stuck a smile on my face and clasped my hands in my lap. "What would you have me talk about?"

"Your brother gave me a beautiful colt. "

I leaned back in the seat. "I saw him. I was there when his mother birthed him. He found his feet fast."

"He has the long legs of a runner. I will race him next year."

"He will be fast and win many races."

A servant brought Pharaoh a glass of wine. He offered one to me. I shook my head. "I have had more than I like already," I murmured.

"I hope the colt is as fast as you and Abram suggest."

I picked up the glass of juice I had been drinking and sipped from it. "Why did you ask about my tapestry?"

"Abram has promised to teach me what he knows about the stars. I want to compare his knowledge with what my fathers taught me. Your tapestry would help to see exactly what he speaks of."

"Yes. I have heard him teach of the stars pointing to my tapestry before. When shall I bring it for your discussion?"

Pharaoh turned toward me. "I hoped you would send it."

"It is a prized possession, taking me many months to complete. I would not want to lose it. And I love hearing Abram talk of the stars. Can I not come with it and see him again?"

"You love your brother?"

I nodded. "Very much. He has protected me for many years." *As my husband and lover.*

He rose. "I will send a servant to help carry the tapestry and lead you to us tomorrow. Be ready after the midday meal."

"I will," I said, standing as well.

He turned on his slippered heel and strode toward the knot of staring women. "Senet, my love," he cooed. "Come with me."

A tall, graceful woman separated herself from the others. With a smile, she took his hand and walked with him out of the room and down a corridor. She never looked in my direction. I pressed my palm to my heart and breathed in deeply. *Not enticed into his bed yet.*

Nabukha returned to her seat beside me. "He left already?"

"Is that unusual? Does he usually expect a new woman to bed him?"

"Not normally. He usually marries the woman before bedding her, but not always."

I sighed. "Good. I feared he might bed me."

Nabukha laughed softly. "He will, but not yet. He wants you to be comfortable here first."

"Will I ever be comfortable here?" I murmured.

"I do not know. I hope so. It is helpful to be one of Pharaoh's favorites."

When I returned to my rooms, I found my baskets and bags sitting in the middle of the room. I opened the basket holding my tapestries and looked through them. My star tapestry lay on the top. I pulled it out and held it close to my body. Tears leaked from my eyes.

Abram. Oh, Abram. I miss you so.

I opened another basket to find a comfortable sleeping robe. I pulled my favorite one out and gathered it into my arms, inhaling Abram's fragrance. Tears continued to leak down my cheeks.

My door opened and a young dark-haired woman, dressed in a short, straight shift stepped through.

"Who are you?" I asked, hurriedly wiping my eyes with my sleeping robe.

The woman dropped her eyes. "I am Hagar. I was assigned as your servant."

"Servant? Why? Who did that?"

"Everyone who comes here receives a servant. Yafeu assigned me to you," Hagar said in a rush. She took a deep breath and let it out. "Senet sent me away thinking Yafeu would banish me from the palace, but Yafeu has responsibility for the servants, not Senet." A tear dripped off her nose.

I touched her arm. "I am grateful you came to help me. I left my servant with our other people."

"Oh, thank you." She fell to her knees at my feet. "Yafeu says he will send me into the city if you send me away. Please do not send me away."

I knelt in front of her with my eyebrows drawn close together. "Why did Senet send you away?"

Hagar glanced up into my eyes, then dropped them to the floor again. "I did not ... did not ... warn her ..."

"Warn her? Of what?"

"The other girl who served Senet with me lay with her husband and I did not share. She says I betrayed her trust, says Pharaoh would want to bed me next."

"And do you want that?"

"No, mistress. I want to find a man to marry. Only my husband will bed me."

I stood and pulled her to her feet. "Hagar, I will not send you away unless you are unfaithful to me. Keep everything you learn about me to yourself and share none of it."

Hagar sobbed. "Mistress, I will do everything you say. I will keep anything I learn about you to myself."

I patted her back. "Then we will get along. Will you help me with my sleeping robe, then take these loops out of my hair?"

She wiped her nose on the back of her hand. I opened the bag hanging across my body and found a square of cotton, which I handed to her. "Use this."

She took it and blew her nose. She helped pull the sleeping robe over my head and pull it straight. "That is beautiful, but it is so ... long."

"It is the way I like it."

"I prefer shorter sleeping robes. Sit in front of the mirror. I will help you with your hair."

I perched on the stool in front of the table below the polished brass mirror and Hagar took the jeweled combs from my hair, setting them on the table. "Are these beautiful combs yours?"

I shook my head. "No. Ami and Sanura put them in my hair. We need to find them and return them."

"They are beautiful. I will find Ami and Sanura in the morning."

Hagar brushed my hair with a brush left on the table. Its stiff boar hair bristles swept through my hair and the tangles caused by the loops. She patiently brushed through the tangles when the brush bounced across the tangles.

"Will you want to sleep late in the morning?" she asked.

I shook my head, enjoying the feel of my hair swishing on my shoulders. Each evening before, I had loosened my hair for the night. This small familiar movement relaxed me. "No. I have a busy day tomorrow. Pharaoh has promised I can go see Abram tomorrow. He needs my tapestry to discuss the stars with Pharaoh."

"Who is this Abram?"

"Abram is ... is my ... is my ... brother. He has done much for me. I love and miss him very much."

"It is good to love your brother. I had a brother ... on the river."

"He did not know how to swim?"

"Yes, he could swim. In a place with this much water, he learned to swim early, although our mother never liked it. She feared the crocodiles. But Nesu loved the water ..." She rolled her lips inward. "But when a child fell into the river, he jumped in to retrieve her."

"How did that happen?"

"Father and Nesu worked on a boat on the Black, transporting grain up the river. The employer brought along his little daughter for the day. She easily rode on top of the load until the barge bumped into something in the middle of the river. She lost her balance and fell into the water. Nesu jumped in and pulled her out."

"Could he not climb back on the boat?" I asked, horror filling my stomach. I set my hand against the stirring in it.

"He got the little girl back on and Father reached to pull him back on. But ..." she bit her lower lip, "Grandfather Sobek got him." Hagar swallowed. "Nesu screamed and Father and the owner beat the crocodile with the long poles they used to propel the barge up and down the river, but it did not let go."

I set my hand against my mouth, holding back my cries. "That is worse than I expected it to be." I whimpered. "Did you see it?"

Hagar ducked her head, then lifted it to braid my hair for sleep. "Yes. We gathered papyrus on the banks of the river when their barge hit the enormous crocodile." She closed her eyes and swallowed once more. "Nesu was older than me. He protected me from the bullies who lived near us and warned me about Pharaoh's men who hunted young girls. After his ... accident, Pharaoh's men found me alone and brought here. Nesu was not there to protect me from them."

"Your poor mother and father, to lose a son in that way, then lose you to Pharaoh's household."

"It is not as bad for them to lose me. Pharaoh pays them some each month for my service here." Hagar lifted a shoulder. She tied a string around my braid to hold it in place.

"What do you get from Pharaoh for your service?"

"Better food than I ever ate at home, nicer clothing than Father and Mother could get for me, and a warm, dry bed to sleep in each night. I do not complain. If Senet were to get her way, and forced Yafeu to put me out, my father and mother would lose their payment for my service. They lost Nesu's support when the ..." she swallowed, "crocodile got him. I could not do that to my parents. I thank you for taking me in."

"I will keep you as long as I am here, but you must remember to keep anything you learn about me to yourself."

"Yes, mistress."

"Do you have a place to sleep?" I turned on the stool to look into her eyes.

"I am to sleep here so I can meet your needs at night."

Abram cannot sneak in to be with me if she is here at night. Would he try? I want him to come see me, but I doubt he will.

"Then we must find a place for you to sleep."

We wandered through my new rooms and found a small side room with a narrow cot.

"This room and bed are for me," Hagar said. "It is prepared for the servant of the woman who occupies this room."

"Then it is yours," I said. "Do you have possessions you need to gather and bring here?"

"They are outside the door." Hagar walked to my door and retrieved a small basket carrying her few possessions.

"That is not much," I said.

"Enough for me. I will retrieve my clothing when Senet is out of her rooms. She would not allow me to take them with me."

"If she refuses to allow you to recover them, we will get you more clothing," I said. I did not know what I would do to get her more clothing, but I would find a way.

Hagar led me to the community bathing rooms the next morning and helped me bathe and dress. She brushed and curled my hair back in our rooms.

After eating our morning meal, I unrolled my tapestry.

"Beautiful," Hagar said. "No wonder your brother wants to use this to teach Pharaoh. I have seen many of these stars."

She helped me to roll it and prepare it to be taken to Pharaoh.

Sometime after our midday meal, a servant came to carry my tapestry and guide me to the room where Abram and Pharaoh met. They discussed stars and numbers. Both men. One I loved, one I did not. One I longed to be with, the other — desired to be with me. My stomach clenched.

"There you are," Abram said.

I longed to feel his arms surrounding me. I desired his kisses. I had not slept well the night before, missing his warmth beside me. I would have to be careful about my feelings.

"How are you?" He gave me a gentle hug and a chaste kiss on the cheek.

I lifted my shoulder. "I did not sleep as well as I could. The bed was too empty," I whispered. Then I spoke louder, "I am good. They have treated me well. You?"

"I missed you last night. Did he bed you?" he whispered in my ear. "They gave me lovely rooms near Lot's and Galya's rooms. We had a delicious meal last night."

I shook my head. "I have a room and a servant to help me. She is helpful."

Pharaoh waved to us. "Come, sit near us while we speak."

I hooked elbows with Abram and joined Pharaoh.

The servant had unrolled my tapestry on an enormous table. As big as it was, the edges hung off it.

"Your tapestry is beautiful," Pharaoh said. "How close does it match the sky?"

"It matches the sky above Moreh exactly," Abram said.

"We went out to look at the night sky many times to ensure my tapestry is exact," I said.

Pharaoh touched some stars. "I know these. I see them above Egypt."

He and Abram bent over the tapestry and discussed the stars. I found a seat a short distance from them and listened to the discussion. Abram and I had often talked about the stars and their placement in the heavens. It was good to hear him share this information.

A servant brought me a tray of cheeses and fruits and a pitcher of cold fruit juice. He took a similar tray to Abram and Pharaoh. They picked up fruit and cheese and ate them without thinking as they argued over the placement of a star.

I leaned back in my chair and soaked in Abram's voice. I did not believe I would miss it so much in just one night. He had left me behind as he traveled to sell the wool from our sheep and goats before. But here, I missed him more than ever before, knowing he slept somewhere nearby in the palace. So close, yet so far from me.

I refused to allow my tears to fall while I was with him. I held them back until later when I was alone. For now, I enjoyed hearing the lilt of his voice.

After three hours, Pharaoh rang a small, tinkling bell. The servant who had guided me to the room hurried from the portico where he waited. At Pharaoh's nod, he rolled my tapestry and lifted it into his arms.

While he did, Abram came to sit next to me. "Will you be safe?" he asked.

"Yafeu, the steward over the women's quarters, watches over his women. No other man, except Pharaoh, may enter the women's quarters."

"Are you alone? I miss you."

"And I miss you. I have a friend, Nabukha. She kept me company when the other women gathered close to Senet and refused to speak with me."

"You may be safer if she ignores you," Abram said. He took my hand and held it as a brother would.

"I would be safest with you," I said, fighting to keep the longing from my voice. "How long will you stay?"

"I do not know. I suppose it will depend on the weather." He squeezed my hand. "If it rains, we can return to Canaan."

"We? How will you get me out of the women's quarter?"

"I will find a way." He rose as Pharaoh came to join us. "My servant has your tapestry ready to take it back to your rooms, unless you want to leave it here with us?"

"I know you like my tapestry, but it is a reminder of our home. I would like to take it back with me."

Pharaoh's smile was cool. "I had hoped you would allow me to keep it to study."

I peeked at Abram, whose head barely shook.

"If I allow you to keep it, you will forget to allow me to listen to your discussions," I said.

"You listened to all that? Did you understand?" Pharaoh asked, his eyebrows rising toward his hair.

"Abram and I have spent many evenings discussing those same things. I understand."

"I do not mind having you join us, although your beauty sometimes causes me to forget what I was saying."

I smiled and tucked a loose lock of hair. "I will sit back a bit if I disturb you. I do like listening to your discussions."

Pharaoh sighed. "No. You come sit with us and join the discussions if you like. I will enjoy having a beautiful woman so near."

I glanced at Abram. He winked at me.

"I will be happy to join your discussion and share my tapestry." I smiled at Abram. "I miss seeing my brother."

"I would love to have a sister who loves to be near me as you love to be near your brother," Pharaoh said.

As he gave me a hug, I peeked over his shoulder at Abram. A sick look filled his face. He did not like Pharaoh to touch me like this any more than I did. He pursed his lips together and smoothed his face, flicking his eyes toward the servant. We had to be careful.

I allowed Pharaoh to kiss me on the cheek before he released me. "My servant will come for you tomorrow. Be ready."

"I will. Will you let me know before he comes?"

"I will send a messenger. Yafeu will let you know."

I walked behind the servant who carried my rolled tapestry. As we turned a corner, my eyes flicked back toward Abram and Pharaoh. Abram stared after me, working to keep his face smooth of emotion in front of Pharaoh. This was as hard for him as it was for me.

Chapter Thirteen

Women's Court

Each day I would receive a message shortly before the servant came to carry my tapestry and guide me to the room where Abram and Pharaoh met. The room changed occasionally. Sometimes we met in a room near the outside of the building with big windows open to the sky three floors up. I would lean out the window and look down on people outside the walls as they carried on their business.

Beggars in ragged shirts leaned against the wall. Some shook their bowls, and some called out in pitiful voices, asking for coins. A few squatted silently, hoping for mercy from passers-by.

People swirled past, moving toward unknown destinations. Men in kilts that swept to their feet escorted women dressed in long shifts. Others whose kilts almost covered the private parts of their bodies carried heavy loads.

Other days, I met the men in an inside room with small windows and lit by beeswax candles that gave off little smoke.

In these different rooms, I listened to the men discuss numbers and stars, gods, and laws. Sometimes I would insert a comment. Most of the time, though, I listened, enjoying my time near Abram.

However, my time with Abram was too short, and I could not speak openly about missing his arms holding me at night. I spent more of my days in the women's quarters with Hagar and the other women. I could not mope in my rooms. They expected me to join the others in the baths in the morning and in the big socializing chamber in the later afternoon.

Many of the women napped during the time I spent with Abram and Pharaoh. They gathered in the afternoon to gossip and eat. I joined Nabukha most afternoons, uninterested in their gossip.

"She fears you will wed Pharaoh and take his interest from her," Nabukha said. "She did it to her older sister."

"Her older sister?" I asked. "Which woman was that?"

"Me. I was once Pharaoh's favorite."

I swallowed. "How can you sit here and watch her hold court?"

"It is her time. I do not mind. I do not want her to get her claws into you. Stay free of Pharaoh."

"That is difficult when he has me join him each afternoon during discussions with Abram." I leaned back, feigning disinterest in the women surrounding Senet. Something about her concerned me. "What can she do to me?"

"She has already tried to remove your servant. But I spoke with Yafeu. I still have some power here. She cannot override my requests, much as she wants."

I blanched. "She would try to hurt me like that?"

"She can try to make things miserable for you. See how she pulls the other women into her circle?" Nabukha flicked her eyes toward the women. "She wants everyone to be part of her admirers. Senet wants to exclude you."

"It does not matter to me. I am not interested in her group or her opinions," I said, flicking my fingers. "I did not choose to be here. There is nothing she can do to me or for me."

"If she learns you want nothing from her and prefer to leave, she will do everything she can to keep you here."

I snorted. "She will not learn unless you tell her or one of her little friends listen in to our conversations."

Nabukha grinned. "Let her wonder about what we say. Her little sycophants will try, but we will keep them wondering. Do not share with anyone, especially your maidservant."

"She has sworn to keep things private." I searched the edge of the room, seeking Hagar among the other maidservants. She sat away from them. "Hagar is not gossiping with the other women."

"Not now. But Senet will pull her in. Hagar aspires to be part of her inner circle. Senet kicked her out once. She will pull her back."

I shook my head. "I will be extra careful. I do so want to leave this place with its intrigues. I liked the simple life at home."

"It is a game we play to stay interested in life," Nabukha said. "What else do we do with our lives?"

"I would love a weaving loom or a needle and thread. I can think of many things to do while sitting here, rather than the boredom of watching Senet." I closed my eyes, seeing the unfinished tasks waiting for my time.

"You know how to weave and sew?" Nabukha asked.

I opened an eye. "Yes. Where I came from, all women learned those arts. I made this dress," I ran my hand above my dress, "and sewed the design."

"I used to sew. I wonder if I still could. We could start something interesting. Do you want to try?"

I glanced at my friend and raised my eyebrows. This could be fun.

"It will make Senet furious," Nabukha said.

"Then we must."

"Tomorrow, when you come, bring your sewing. Surely you have something you are working on?"

"Yes. In my chest. I have a gift for Abram, a special robe for him to wear."

"Bring it tomorrow. I will bring sewing I put aside. We will see what the other women do."

I shook my head and grinned. "You are devious. I assume they never learned to sew?"

"No. Senet does not want to do things her maidservants should be doing. We should invite our maids to join us. Mine sews. Does your Hagar?"

"I do not know, but I will teach her if she does not."

The next afternoon, Nabukha and I gathered in our usual place. We invited our maids to join us. And this time, we did not lounge back in lazy rest. We sat upright with fabric in our laps and needles full of bright thread in our fingers.

Hagar had learned to sew as a child and quickly found a piece of fabric to sew beautiful designs on. She planned to use it as a sash with her shift.

We visited as we sewed. I would occasionally glance at the mob of women giggling around Senet. That first day, they laughed and pointed at us.

"It is as I expect," Nabukha said. "They do not understand what we do, so they jeer. That will change."

Later, when Pharaoh made his usual tour through the women's quarters, he stopped to see what Nabukha and I did.

"That is a beautiful robe," he said to me. "Is it for me?"

I ducked my head. "I am making it as a surprise for my brother. Abram needs a new robe."

"And I thought you cared about me." Pharaoh feigned sadness.

"You have been kind to me and I may make you a robe. But this robe is for Abram. I started it before we arrived here in Memphis."

Pharaoh pouted. "I would like some woman to care enough about me that she would make me something special."

"Perhaps Senet would?" Nabukha suggested.

Pharaoh brightened. "Do you think she would? I have never seen her sew."

"Ask her," Nabukha said, grinning at me.

The next day, I left Abram's robe in my rooms and brought a different length of fabric. I decided Hagar's plan to make a sash would work for me too. Perhaps I would give it to Pharaoh, something he could wear it above his kilt.

I had decided on a masculine pattern using black and red threads. When Pharaoh came in on his nightly tour, I tucked it into my basket and pulled out a skirt to sew pink and purple flowers along the hem. I wanted to surprise him with his sash.

He strode toward Nabukha and me as soon as he saw us in our usual place, ignoring Senet and the other women.

"You are sewing something different. Did you finish the robe for Abram?"

I frowned at him. "No. I did not want to make you sad. I am making this skirt for a special occasion."

He lifted his eyebrows. "Special occasion. Are you planning something I do not know about?"

"No. I just like to have something available if something shows up unexpectedly."

"Like a marriage?" His grin reminded me of the crocodiles in the river.

"Are you going to marry another woman? I thought you love Senet?"

"I do. She is my first wife, after you, Nabukha. But," he waggled his eyebrows, "I could find another favorite."

"Keep Senet. She still offers you much. She is young. Do I see her belly grow?"

Pharaoh's eyes jerked from mine to the circle of women surrounding Senet. "I did not see. I must find out." He strode toward her, her circle of followers barely moving out of his way before he barged past them.

Nabukha grinned. "That was an excellent ploy. He never has enough sons."

"Or daughters?" I asked.

"Oh, he has many daughters. Never enough sons. He will not be happy if Senet is not with child."

"She is. I can see it in her glow. I doubt even she is aware of the child."

"Pharaoh will be happy. He will stop bothering you so much."

"I hope so. I do not want to marry or bed the man."

When I next joined Abram and Pharaoh, Pharaoh was all smiles. "Your sister saw my wife is with child before Senet even knew," he crowed, "she is amazing."

Abram ducked his head. "She is an amazing woman."

"I will give you oxen for her help," Pharaoh cried.

"But I — "

"We thank you for your generosity," Abram said, giving me a look to stop speaking.

"I thank you for your generosity," I said. "But I had nothing to do with Senet becoming with child. That was all you."

Pharaoh's mood was happier than I had seen him since we arrived. "Perhaps he will not want me as a wife now and will let me go?" I whispered to Abram later.

"Perhaps."

I finished the design on the sash I made for Pharaoh and gave it to him when he next entered the women's quarters soon after. As usual, he strode directly to Nabukha and me before going to spend the rest of the evening with Senet.

"You wanted something made just for you. I cannot present you with a child, but perhaps this sash will suffice?" I presented the sash to him with a bow.

He fingered the stitching and examined the pattern. "So manly. Where do I wear it? On my head?" He held it to his forehead. "Across my body?" He draped it from his shoulder to his waist.

"I thought you could wear it above your kilt," I suggested. "The sash is yours to wear any way you wish."

He bent and kissed me on the cheek. "You have surprised me once more. I will honor you with more asses."

"Give them to my brother. Abram can care for them while I am here," I said.

He tipped his head back and laughed, then walked to Senet to show her his gift.

"Why does he do that?" I asked Nabukha.

"What? Laugh with you, then go to Senet?"

"No. He always comes first to speak with you and me."

"He still honors me as his first wife, even though I am no longer his favorite wife. My womb is old and no longer gives him sons and daughters. Senet's does."

I nodded. That seemed appropriate. No wonder Senet glared at us as Pharaoh entered our quarters. She fears another old woman will take Pharaoh's attention from her.

"How did you make that ... that sash for Pharaoh? Teach me?" Senet begged the next afternoon.

"Do you have lengths of linen or threads of many colors?" I asked.

"No." Senet stared at her hands with a frown. Then her face lit up. "But I can ask Yafeu to bring me some. Then will you teach me?"

"Request a sharp needle as well," Nabukha suggested, holding hers up. "You cannot sew without a needle."

The following afternoon, Senet gleefully showed us her sewing supplies. She sounded like a giggly little girl, rather than the queen of Egypt.

Most of the women also joined us with the needed materials to learn to sew. Nabukha and I gave them simple instructions. Senet's fingers were fastest to learn their new use. She crowed when Nabukha told her she learned fast.

After that, Senet's circle of women often joined us to sew. After they became more confident, they would sometimes return to their original place, but more often they stayed with us, sharing gossip of the palace.

Pharaoh often found reason to award sheep, camels, asses, donkeys, and goats to Abram for something I said or did from then on. Abram's wealth had doubled since arriving in Memphis. I was happy for him but missed him terribly. I wanted to sleep next to him. I wanted Abram to bed me and give me a child.

One afternoon, Senet did not join us.

"Where is our lady, Senet?" Nabukha asked the women who followed her.

"Did you not hear?" one replied. "She has taken to her bed with a sickness. The child is still within her, but ..."

I gasped. "How long has she been ill?"

"Since last night. The healer is with her, but he fears for the child."

I hurried away to my rooms and closed the door. I knelt in the middle of the room and begged Jehovah to save Senet's baby. I had no desire to see her suffer as I had suffered.

When I looked up, Hagar sat next to me. Her face had lost its color. "You are one of those?" she said, her voice almost accusing me.

"One of those what?" I asked.

"Part of the Jehovah cult."

I swallowed the sudden thickness in my throat. "It is not a cult. But, yes. I worship Jehovah. He is my God and has protected me many times and abundantly blessed me."

"Can Jehovah save Senet's babe?" she asked.

I gawked into her eyes a long moment. He had not saved my babe. "He can, if He chooses to bless her and Pharaoh in that way."

"Then I will join you in your prayers. I do not believe Elkenah can save the child's life. That so-called god can only take away the lives of our children."

I nodded. Hagar knelt so her feet were against the door to prevent a disturbance to our prayers for the safety of the child and for Senet.

Almost two hours later, Yafeu pounded on my door. When Hagar opened it, he waited impatiently with three male bearers. "Pharaoh demands you leave immediately."

"Does he want me to come to a meeting with him and Abram?" I asked.

Yafeu stomped his foot. "No. You and your husband are to leave Memphis. Gather your things and go now."

My jaw dropped. I quickly closed my mouth. "Husband? Who is —"

"We know you are married to Abram. He admitted it to Pharaoh. These men are here to carry your possessions."

"Can I have a few minutes to repack?" I asked. Most of my possessions still lay in the baskets and bags. "It should not take long."

Yafeu nodded. "A very few minutes."

Hagar leapt to her feet to help me.

"You must gather your possessions, Hagar," Yafeu said. "Pharaoh has given you as a handmaid to Sarai. You will leave with her."

Leave with me? What disaster have I brought on Hagar's head?

"Leave here? This is my home!" Hagar cried.

"It was your home. Not anymore. Your home is wherever Abram and Sarai take you."

She sucked in a deep breath and rushed to the little room she had occupied since that first evening when I arrived in the women's quarters. While I gathered my possessions and packed them into my bags and baskets, Hagar did the same.

"What about these combs?" I asked Hagar, holding the combs placed in my hair that first day. "Did you try to return them to Ami and Sanura?"

"I did. Ami says they are yours, a gift from Pharaoh."

I took them to Yafeu. "Do you want these back?"

He took the combs and turned them over in his hands. "No. Pharaoh gave these to you. They are yours. Put them in your bag. Do you have everything yet?"

"Almost."

I checked to ensure that my clothing, previously sent to the laundry, hung on the clothing pegs before turning to Yafeu and his men. "I am ready."

Hagar returned from her small room with a smaller basket of possessions. "I am ready to go. Are you certain Pharaoh gave me to Sarai?"

"I am certain. Your life is now in her hands."

Yafeu ordered the men to carry our bags and baskets, then turned on his heel. "Follow me."

He led the way through the now familiar corridors and out of the women's quarters. Hagar paused at the door and turned back. "I had a comfortable life here."

"I hope you find life with us as pleasant," I said, gently touching her arm. "We are decent people."

I hoped to see Nabukha in the halls so I could bid her farewell, but we saw no one. They must still be in the women's socializing chamber. I would miss her wisdom.

We met Abram on the steps outside Pharaoh's palace. I fell into his arms and felt his warm, loving arms surround me again. "I missed you. But how did Pharaoh find out about us?"

"He said he heard from an angel who warned him he could not take you as his wife. Jehovah would plague his household until he returned you to me."

"He will not kill you for me?"

"No. We have had too many valuable conversations about the stars, planets, and numbers, even Jehovah. He will not kill me. But he will no longer allow us to stay within the boundaries of his lands. Pharaoh commanded us to leave."

"He gave Hager to me as a handmaid. His anger must not be terrible."

"He gave me men servants as well. He begged me not to call more disasters onto his house. His fathers worshiped Jehovah even when they were not allowed the Priesthood of God. He asked that I pray for his favorite wife, Senet."

"We prayed for her this afternoon. Has she healed yet?" I asked.

"It is in Jehovah's hands. I, too, prayed for Senet and her child. Pharaoh has treated us well. He deserves this child."

Danil and our other herders met us as we reached the gate, leading our camels. Bara took Hagar, leading her to join the other women in the caravan.

Soon, our company had left Pharaoh's gates and wended our way out of Memphis. Once more, we would travel to Canaan. I hoped the drought and famine had ended.

Chapter Fourteen

Leaving Egypt

It took Hagar some time to acclimate herself to life on the trail. She had spent much of the last years in the women's quarters. The dirt and dust left her in tears.

I embraced her the first evening and allowed her to cry. "I thought I would see my mother and father again. Now I will not. They will never see me again, and never know what happened to me."

"We can send them a letter — tell them you are with us."

"We could, but neither Mother nor Father read."

"And no one in their neighborhood reads?"

"No. I did not read until I went to the palace."

Abram touched Hagar's back. "I know your parents depend on the coins Pharaoh sent. I sent men to find your parents."

"Did they find them?" Hagar cried.

Abram nodded. "They did, and they left a bag of coins with them and told them you are leaving with us."

Hagar embraced Abram and sobbed once more.

When she calmed, Bara showed Hagar the tent for servants, leaving Abram and me alone for the first time in many weeks.

Abram dropped the door closed to our tent and gathered me into his arms. "I have missed you so much. It killed me to tell Pharaoh you were my sister. What would I do if he had bedded you?"

"That was my greatest fear. How could I avoid breaking my marriage covenants when Pharaoh thought of me as your sister?"

"You did not?" he asked, kissing my face and lips.

"No. He came to see me and Nabukha first each evening when he came into the women's quarters. I feared he would want to bed me. But Nabukha told me he would not try to take me until we married. I found reasons to keep him interested in Senet rather than me." I clung to him, savoring his touch, his smell, his kisses.

"He said you pointed out her glow." He kissed me again.

"I have wanted a child for so long. I see it when a woman first becomes with child." I chewed on the inside of my lip. "It has become something I see, always wishing someone would see it in me."

"It will happen," Abram comforted. "Jehovah promised us a large family."

"When?" I wailed. "I am an old woman. Almost past the time when I can bear a child. Soon my womb will dry and it will never be possible for me to carry a child."

Abram caressed me. "We can try again now. I missed being with you."

"And I missed you. Nighttime and bed were so lonely alone."

"Never again, Sarai. I will not ask you to pretend to be my sister again." His kisses became ardent.

Later, as we lay together in our bed, he shared with me what had happened.

"This morning, Pharaoh called me to come immediately to his rooms. I looked for you, thinking he had called me to come discuss numbers again."

"I was not called."

"I know. Pharaoh paced the room in front of me, raging at me. How could he trust me in other things? I had misled him. I had brought a plague on his house. He had considered taking you as his wife. His beloved favorite wife, Senet, lay in bed, struggling to keep their child within her." Sorrow mixed with joy in his voice.

"How did he find out? I did not say or do anything to cause him to think we were more than brother and sister."

"We were careful. We did not give him reason to believe anything else. As he prayed for the safety of Senet and the child, an angel came to him."

"He prayed to Jehovah?"

"He said he did. His family has believed in Jehovah since his ancient grandmother founded and settled Egypt. But, as a son of Ham and Canaan, his fathers lost the privilege of serving Jehovah with the priesthood."

I inhaled deeply. "What did the angel tell Pharaoh?"

"He was told a plague had come to his household because he considered taking you as his wife. The angel told him we were married, and it would cause you to commit adultery if he bedded you." He kissed me once more. "He gave me silver, gold, and many animals if we would leave his lands immediately. He also gave me herders and servants. I am now truly a Prince of Ur and Canaan."

I gazed at Abram sitting with his head against the pillows, seeing the man I had missed so deeply for so long. "Yes. But for me, you will always be my King."

Abram grinned. "And you are my Queen. How did you keep Pharaoh away from you?"

"I turned his interest toward Senet. I did all I could to keep him happy with you and still not be interested in taking me as his wife."

"Since Senet carried his child, he decided he needed a new wife until after the child came. He planned to marry you today. He said you already had sewn a special dress. He thought you wanted to marry him."

I allowed a grin to fill my face. "I made a special dress, but I made it to wear when we were alone together once more. I did not have time to put it on this evening."

"Tomorrow will be soon enough, my love," Abram crooned.

I pushed back his arm from me. "I have something for you."

He tried to pull me back. "It can wait. It has waited all these weeks."

I wanted him to know I had thought of him in my absence, that I needed to be with him. I tried to move away from his arms, but he overcame me. "Tomorrow, then," I said, falling back beside him and letting him encircle me with his arms once more.

"Sarai. Sarai. I have missed you so. I never want to let you out of my sight again."

His words warmed my soul. "And I never want to leave you again. But you will go to the hills and pastures with the animals. You will leave to sell our wool."

"But you will always be mine. I do not want to lose you to another man."

"And I will never desire to be given to another man. You are my husband. I belong to you, heart, soul, and body."

We lay together whispering words of love late into the night. I lay clasped in his arms even the next morning. I had missed him so much. I did not want to move for any reason, but we would need to move on. We could not stay within Pharaoh's lands.

I slipped out of Abram's arms and left the bed. After pulling on a clean dress and robe for the day, I found the robe I made for Abram while I waited for Pharaoh to let me go.

Carrying it to the bed, I stared at my beautiful man. Even at nearly eighty, his hair shone dark and thick. I bent to kiss him awake.

"There you are. I dreamed we were parted." Abram pulled me onto the bed in a tight caress.

"We were. But Jehovah brought me forth. I am yours once more." I returned his searching kisses.

When I lifted my head, gasping for air, I pulled the robe from between us. "I made this for you. You should rise and put it on. It is past dawn and we have far to travel."

Abram perched on the bed and examined the robe. "You made this for me while in Pharaoh's palace?"

"I made it earlier. I could not weave there. But I added the design along the edges."

"And Pharaoh thought it was for him?" He lifted his eyebrows in question.

"He did. After that, I made a sash for him, working on your robe only in my rooms. I did not want him to take what is yours." I bent to kiss him.

He gently pulled me close and kissed me deeply.

"Abram? Abram?" Lot called from outside our tent door. "I know you two are awake. We must be leaving soon. Pharaoh's guards are getting restless."

Abram sighed deeply. "I want to spend all day with you alone. But we must move on."

He flipped back the blanket and stepped to the tent door. "I will be out soon."

Lot and Galya joined us and all our friends and followers of Jehovah in their joy of leaving Egypt. They had grown tired of life controlled by Pharaoh and desired the freedom to live and serve Jehovah.

I cherished my time with Abram as we retraced the trail we had traveled months ago on our way to Egypt. It took much longer to traverse back to Canaan, as our herds had expanded. Besides all the animals given to us by Pharaoh in the time we lived in Egypt, our ewes and she-goats had borne little ones, many with twins.

We stopped in Sichem to offer sacrifices to Jehovah in gratitude for his protection, before returning to Moreh and our earlier home site.

Abram and Lot pitched our tents and we settled in. I reveled in the comfortable hills that surrounded us. No one could take me from Abram.

The drought had ended in the time we were gone to Egypt, and green grass filled the hills and meadows. That first morning, I stood outside our tent and watched the herders scatter into the hills with the animals. They filled the land.

Hagar helped Galya with her daughter. They became close. It made me happy to see Hagar make friends. I had taken her from her home.

We returned to Moreh and had only settled there a little more than two months when Danil came to Abram.

"We have a problem," Danil said.

I brought him a cool drink and rested near the walls of the tent with my spinning spindle to listen to them speak. Hagar stayed nearby, spinning thread.

"What is the problem?" Abram asked.

"Our herds are too large."

Abram's eyebrows bounced upward. "Too large? How can that be?"

"There is not enough greenery for them all. Already our herders contend with Lot's herders. They almost came to blows today. If we do not change something soon, there will be fights over the best land."

"I never thought our wealth and all our animals would cause us problems," Abram said. He set his head in his hand. "I will discuss the problem with Jehovah first, then with Lot. We cannot have anyone hurt because of our wealth."

"I knew you would find a way to solve it," Danil said as he left the tent.

"We should ask Lot and Galya to join us for our dinner," Abram said.

I agreed. "Hagar, please go invite Lot and Galya to eat with us this evening?"

She nodded and set down her spinning and walked out the tent door.

"It is good you have Hagar to help you," Abram said. "Yael has much to do with her new son."

I sighed softly. Even Yael had a child. I did not. "Yes, she is too busy to be my maid. I am grateful Pharaoh gave Hagar to me."

"Have you spoken with her about her beliefs?"

"She joined me in praying for Senet. Since we left Egypt, she has not asked many questions. When she first discovered me praying for Senet, she referred to our beliefs as a cult."

"Perhaps we should consider teaching her?" Abram's voice was a gentle chiding.

I ducked my head. I had not considered teaching her. "I will teach her."

"If you need help —" Abram suggested.

"I will ask," I answered.

Hagar returned shortly after. "Galya said she and Lot would be happy to join you for dinner. She said they had considered inviting you."

"Lot is seeing the same problems," Abram murmured.

In the days after Egypt, Yael had spent time with Hagar. She taught her to cook on the trail and in a camp home, something she had not needed to do in the women's quarters of Pharaoh's palace. She had cooked with her mother before the soldiers of Pharaoh took her away. Hagar had a small tent pitched near our larger one and now spent most of her days helping me.

"It is good that I planned a larger dinner for tonight," she said.

She stepped out to the fire and checked the dinner.

I joined her. "Would you like me to help with something?"

"No, mistress. I would like to show you how much I have learned. I never thought I could cook and help a lady like you when the guards took me to the women's court."

"You have learned fast."

"I appreciate the opportunity to learn," Hagar said. "And space to be alone. I have never had that before."

"You are welcome to it. You are a tremendous help to me. But if you change your mind …"

"I will call you." She flipped her hair back and bent over her cooking.

I returned to the tent and found our best dishes and a cloth to put on the table. Although the purpose for the dinner could be difficult, we could continue to show love for each other.

Later that evening, Galya, Lot, and their daughter came to dinner. Hagar served the food she had prepared and gladly accepted our praise.

After eating, we women moved to one side of the tent while the men relaxed in our comfortable chairs. We spoke softly about weaving, cooking, and other women's chores while listening to the men. If the problems were not for us to hear, they would leave the tent.

"Lot," Abram said. "Danil tells me we have a problem."

"I heard our herders are arguing about who gets to take their animals to the best meadows," Lot replied.

"We have many more animals than when we lived here before. We need to stop these arguments," Abram said. "The men have come close to blows as they argue about who gets to take their animals where. We cannot have arguments between us. We are brothers."

"I agree, Uncle," Lot said. "What can we do about this?"

"Come with me," Abram said.

The two men walked out into the evening air. Galya and I followed, wondering what the men would do to solve this problem.

Abram waved his hands out to indicate the land in front of them.

"There is much land here. Many places for us to go with our animals. There is no reason for strife between us."

"Beautiful land everywhere," Lot agreed. "But the herders believe some is better than others. What will we do?"

Abram sucked in a breath loud enough for me to hear. "We must separate our households and our herds."

How will they do that? Will we move apart? I will not see Rona become a woman or the unborn child Galya carries. Will I see my sister, Galya, again? The problems of too many animals are almost too much to bear.

"How will we do that?" Lot voiced my question.

Abram held his hand in front of him. "Choose. If you go left, I will go right. If you choose right, I will go left. Which direction will you take?"

I looked out at the land in front of us. I loved this plain, but their decision would force us both to leave. Which way would I choose?

The land toward Jordan was verdant and well watered. I thought, if it were my choice, I would divide the plain and take half, giving half to Lot. What would he do?

Galya took my hand. We waited silently near the tent.

"I will take my flocks and my family east toward Jordan."

I wanted to cry out my complaint. Jordan had the best grass and the best water. I looked west toward Canaan. The green of the land appeared browner than the land east in Jordan.

But Abram took Lot by the hand. "It will be as you request. I will move to the west. You move east. I will miss you."

"And I will miss you, Uncle." Lot threw his arms around Abram.

Behind the men, Galya embraced me. "I will miss you, Sarai. You have been more than an auntie to me. You have been a mother."

I have been a mother to Galya and perhaps even other women, but I am unable to carry a child in my womb. I will miss Galya.

"Come see us some time," I said, choking back my tears.

I never considered that the extra wealth we received in Egypt would force us to separate.

Early the next morning, we woke early and loaded our possessions once more onto the backs of camels and donkeys. We embraced Galya, Lot, and their daughter and mounted once more. We turned west toward Canaan.

"I fear for Lot," Abram said as we rode away from the rising sun.

"Why would you fear for them?" I asked. "He took the best land."

"But it is near Sodom. Those men are wicked sinners. I fear their sins will entice him."

"Lot is a righteous man," I said. "He will stay strong."

"I pray you are correct," Abram said.

We rode for three days until we reached the plain of Mamre. After setting up our tents, Abram took Danil and some other men to build an altar.

As he sacrificed a pure male lamb, I watched the rite from a seat near the altar. Hagar sat beside me, asking questions. I shared with her the purpose and meaning of each of Abram's movements.

"Your Jehovah protects you?" she asked.

"He kept me safe from Pharaoh in his palace. He never tried to bed me."

"That is true. I wondered how you avoided that."

"Jehovah protected me as He protected Abram."

"Have you heard anything from Memphis? Did Senet and her child survive?"

"A trader we passed yesterday told us that Senet gave birth to a healthy baby boy in the spring."

"Jehovah be praised," Hagar said. "I know we prayed for her. I did not know Jehovah could heal her and keep her baby safe."

"He did."

As we watched Abram complete the sacrifice, I felt the warmth of Jehovah's spirit fill my heart. He had accepted our sacrifice.

Each day Hagar and I spoke of our belief in Jehovah and his commandments. She slowly came to believe as we did and became one with us in worshiping Jehovah.

Chapter Fifteen

Battle of Giants

Our herds of animals continued to grow, as did our numbers of men and women who became part of our family, our herders, servants, and believers in Jehovah.

The days of my fertility ended. I went months with no suggestion of womanly bleeding. Although I enjoyed the freedom from the challenges of submitting to the bleeding, I realized there would be no children for Abram from me. Through tears and sorrow, I suggested he take another woman as a second wife, but he refused.

"But you must have an heir," I said one evening after he refused once more. "I will not be giving you children. Outsiders will fight over all this," I waved my hand, "if you have no heir."

"Then I will name Danil's son, Eliezer, to be my heir. I will not set you aside for another. Nothing is impossible for Jehovah."

He had spoken. Nothing I said would change his mind.

Four years after our return from Egypt, we faced another challenge. In the surrounding lands, men gathered to battle King Chedorlaomer, who had formed an alliance and demanded tribute from all the kings of the lands in Canaan. This king had even subjugated the king of Sodom. They chafed under his demands and gathered together to battle against him.

They sent messages to us warning of the battle to come, reminding us that the large men, often called giants, were among those who fought on both sides.

Abram chose to stay away. This king did not affect his lands. He paid no tribute.

Word of the battle raging near the Siddim or Salt Sea brought stories of horror as men died terrible deaths. Our herders kept the animals within paddocks to protect them from the wandering armies that would take what they wanted. Vast armies required many animals to feed them. Abram did not choose to make his available to them.

I shuddered outside our tent home, listening to the clash of men echoing across the hills one day after the battle had begun.

Abram took my hand, comforting me. "I will not join in the battle. Jehovah protects us from the horror."

I laid my head against his chest. "Good. I do not want to lose you to war."

Then, the sound of battle silenced. The war had finally ended. Our herders took the animals into the hills to feed on fresh, green grass once more. I prayed that our loved ones outside Sodom were safe.

Life slowly returned to the normal flow. Animals fed in lush green meadows. Women spun the wool into thread and wove fabric.

And then, an injured man stumbled into our camp.

Abram ran to lift him up and called for wine to refresh him. I hurried with the wine and helped him to drink.

Abram and a manservant carried the man to the shade of our tent's overhang and lay him on a blanket.

When the man, Zed, rested enough, he shared a frightening story.

"The battle raged for days. Some days, we thought we would win, with the giants battling for us on our side. Other days, the giants who fought for King Chedorlaomer pushed us back until we feared they would kill us all."

Zed took a sip of the wine in his hands. "It was bloody. Our arrows did little to pierce the skin of the giants. We had to hit them in the eye to cause any damage."

He stopped to shake his head and clutch his arms to his chest. "When they grabbed hold of one of us," he shuddered, "they would shake us upside down, or swing our bodies against the rocks. We had no chance against them."

Tears leaked from his eyes as he spoke. "I ducked as one grabbed for me. He got my friend, Majid, who fought near me and did not see him in time to duck. The giant grasped Majid by the arm and swung him."

Zed choked back a sob. "It was an ugly death."

I tried not to imagine that death. I twisted my hands in my lap, bile burning the back of my throat as I listened to his horror-filled story.

"After days of fighting against them, with our giants falling to theirs, they crowded us into a knot of men on the shore of the Siddim. Our defense collapsed. We could not overcome them and raised our hands in defeat."

Zed bowed his head and sobbed. Abram allowed him time to mourn, then gently pressed for more answers.

"What happened then?"

"They surrounded us and pushed us into a corral as if we were cattle. Our kings could do nothing for us. I do not know where they went. Many hid among us, trying to blend in as mere soldiers. I suspect some ran to the mountains." He took another gulp of the wine. "We waited in those animal corals for three days with little food or water."

"Then what?" Abram asked, nudging Zed to continue his story.

Zed lifted his wine cup to his mouth and found it empty. He stretched it toward Hagar, who held the jug. She filled his cup, and he slurped more of it, spilling some across the front of his torn and bloody tunic.

"People began to arrive from the cities, pushed forward in tight knots, guarded by the giants. Camels and donkeys carried gold and silver from the treasuries and food and other goods from their stores of supplies."

Zed swallowed, paused, then swallowed again. "My family was among the prisoners from Sodom. All but my aged mother and a young daughter because they had succumbed to the vile treatment of their captors."

He eyed his cup of wine and drained it. "I will not share how they died. It is too horrible to remember." He stopped speaking and inhaled several breaths, slowly allowing the air to escape. "It is better they went to live with the gods."

I ducked my head and leaned slightly away from Zed. *How could he survive such vile treatment? How could anyone?*

"Lot? What of Lot? Did he escape?" Abram asked.

Zed shook his head. "They took Lot and his family as prisoners, along with all the others, from in and around Sodom."

I gasped. *Galya and their daughters taken?* I covered my mouth and ducked my head.

"When they had emptied all the cities," Zed continued, "they pulled out their whips to push us out of the corral and up the road toward Damascus. I do not know what King Chedorlaomer and the kings who supported him plan to do with the captives. Sell them. Use the women. I do not know." He stared at Abram. "I am sorry. I left Lot with those murderers."

"How did you escape?" Abram asked.

"Lot found me one day and told me to watch for a chance to escape. If I did, he implored me to come find you. He insisted you would come to rescue him and avenge the loss of so many people."

Abram nodded. "And you escaped?"

Zed nodded and straightened his back. "Late one night, when they had pushed us into a cave so they could drink a stash of wine they found, I walked along the edge, hoping not to be seen. Even the guards had been drinking and were not as watchful as they should have been. They staggered. Another man tried to slip past … and died for his efforts. I could not stay there and watch our people die and be sold off as slaves. Lot's injunction to find you rang in my ears."

He took a deep breath. "The guards had separated and the one giant close to me staggered with his wine. He must have drunk barrels of it."

Abram glared at him. "And?"

"When he turned to march the other way, I slipped past him. I felt the rush of wind from his fingers brushing past me as I ran. I did not stop running until I knew no one was following me. The giant must have kept my escape to himself, rather than be disciplined by his leaders."

Abram rubbed his beard and nodded. "And you came here?"

"I did. I fell many times. They did not feed us enough to have the strength to run or fight back. I ate whatever I could find — insects, plants, an occasional mouse — to maintain the little strength I had."

I waved to Hagar. "He needs food," I whispered.

She bowed and retreated to the cooking fire. When she returned, she brought a bowl of stew and handed it to Zed, who took the bowl and ravenously slurped it down, slowing only to chew on the mutton.

As Zed ate, Abram beckoned me to join him and led me away from our tent.

"I must go rescue Lot and his family," he said.

"Alone? Against so many ..., and giants?"

"Jehovah will be with me. He has promised me safety."

My stomach flipped. How could he think he could win against so many?

"Only with Jehovah's help," Abram said, reading my doubts on my face. "He will support me."

I closed my eyes and lifted my trembling fingers to his brow. "Jehovah bless you," I prayed.

Over the next day, Abram armed our young men he had trained in defense against bears, wolves, and robbers. Now they would use those skills to free Lot and the others.

I paced in front of the tent as he assigned the men to squads and fighting groups, wishing he did not need to leave me. He and Danil spoke late into the night with Zed, learning all they could of the kings and the giants.

Abram slipped into our bed long after I gave up on him and tried to sleep. He held me close and whispered his love for me. Neither one of us slept. The knot in my stomach hardened and I felt I would never eat again.

Early the next morning, I huddled with Hagar, Bara, and the other women watching our young men follow Abram down the road toward Damascus. Would I ever see these men again? Would Abram embrace me once more?

Eliezer stood tall beside his mother. Abram had given him the responsibility of caring for our animals and the people in Mamre. As Abram's heir, he could not join the battle.

Soon after the men and their glinting swords disappeared over the crest of the hill, Eliezer called to the remaining herders and sent the animals out to feed.

Before I knew it, the noise in our camp had been reduced to the whisper of a breeze against the tents. All the men were gone. Then little boys, too young to fight, picked up sticks and ran around pretending to battle the giants and free the captured men of Canaan. Their little voices carried on the breeze, chilling my heart. *Why do our young have to learn warfare so early?*

Our days returned to a semblance of normal. The older men, too old to fight, herded animals out to graze in the morning and brought them home to their paddocks at night. Women spun the wool and wove it between cooking and cleaning their homes, preparing for the return of their men.

I knew Abram would not return soon. He had to catch up to the horde of enemies before he could fight against them. My stomach churned every time I thought of the coming battle. Would a giant catch my Abram and smash his head against the rocks? I could not think of it.

I spent many hours in prayer, and when I spun and wove, I continued in silent prayer for the safety of Abram and our men.

After three weeks, men from other lands drifted back past our home encampment with stories of their release. *They must have made them up, for how could Abram and 318 men have done such things?* I shook my head and waited for Abram to return and share his story with me.

Each time these small groups of men passed us, our women would ask about their men.

"Your men are safe. The enemy killed none," the freed captives would cry. "Their god carried them in His arms and protected them."

I knew he would, but when I learned Jehovah had protected and saved my Abram, I fell to my knees in a prayer of thanksgiving.

Three weeks later, we saw dust rising above the hills. The children ran from where they played on the hill with shouts that our men had returned. Women ran to their stores of food and began enormous pots of stew. Eliezer called for three cattle to be slaughtered. These soon hung over huge cooking fires, waiting for our men.

Soon our men appeared on the road at the top of the hill. Their swords still glinted at their sides. Abram rode ahead of them on his white horse, with Danil, Aner, Eshcol, and Amir, the leaders of the young men, following on their horses.

The young men led donkeys laden with spoils, given to them by the captive kings. The kings had divided the riches taken from the kings who supported King Chedorlaomer. Abram returned with our young men, not spoils or riches.

"I will not have the kings of Sodom or Gomorrah or the other lands say I took from them, nor that they made me wealthy. I took nothing from the spoils of our victory, but gave it to the kings," he said when I asked him where his spoils were.

I clasped Abram in my arms and held him close. "I care not for the spoils of war, nor gold and silver. I care only for you."

"And I care for you, Sarai, my love. Tonight, when we are once again alone, I will share all with you, but now we must celebrate with our young men."

Later, with a bowl of stew and a hunk of beef in our hands, Abram and I strolled through the noise of the celebration. Young men pounded Abram's back, while the women clutched his hands and cried their joy at the return of their men.

I heard snatches of stories from the men.

"Divided us ..."

"Sent us in at night ..."

"Not expecting so few men ..."

"Surprised ..."

"Slaughter ..."

"Covered with blood ..."

"Even the kings ..."

I shuddered at the violence that Abram and his men must have employed to win the lives of Lot and our family back. I did not want to hear. It was too horrible. I slipped away to offer a prayer of gratitude to Jehovah for returning Abram to my arms.

Abram found me in our sleeping space, praying. He knelt and offered his prayers of thanksgiving with me. Then, he took me by the hand and led me out to sit in front of our tent and observe the dancing and joy of our people.

"We must show them we care for them," Abram reminded me.

I only wanted to hold him in my arms. I did not want him to leave me ever again.

Chapter Sixteen

Choice

Late that night, Abram held me tight in his arms, sharing the story. He could tell I did not want to hear of the battle, so he shortened it.

"I followed the spirit. We divided into three groups and surrounded the enemy late at night. They were sleeping off all the wine they had drank the day before. And Jehovah kept them asleep."

I snuggled closer into his arms. "That would make it easier for your small army to defeat them."

"It did. It was a slaughter. Jehovah commanded we kill them all." His voice dropped so low I could almost hear it. "So we did."

"All? Even all the giants?" My heart beat wildly.

"All." He swallowed loudly.

"It must have been ugly," I whispered.

His chin bounced against the top of my head as he nodded. "Yes," he said with a gulp. "I do not take any pride in it, only that I obeyed the word of Jehovah and rescued Lot."

"And the other kings and all their men," I added.

"Yes. Them, too. The rescued kings were happy to have their silver and gold and other goods back. They wanted me to take a portion as my payment. Before we left, Jehovah warned me not to take any for myself. I asked that they give food to my men and a portion of the spoils to the three leaders of the men."

"We have plenty. I am grateful that you returned to me."

"I met Melchizedek, the righteous Prince of Peace, and offered my tithes to Jehovah through him."

"You have been wanting to do that. Is he majestic?"

Abram shook his head. "Yes, but he is the most humble man I have met. He is a man of God. He taught me things I needed to know. Our journey to save Lot was a means for me to meet and learn from one of Jehovah's prophets."

"It must have been wonderful to be in his presence."

I had heard about Melchizedek. An amazing man. If only ...

"I wanted you to be there to meet him," Abram said, answering my unspoken desire. "His wife welcomed me and asked about you."

Breath caught in my throat. "She asked about me? How would she know?"

"Word has spread about us. I do not know how or why. We are but simple herders."

"Simple, but with a large community about us."

"True enough. But the most humbling experience came in the night when Jehovah spoke with me again."

I turned so I could see his face. "He has spoken to you before."

"Yes, but this was different. Jehovah taught me many important things about this earth, its beginning, and how it will end." His voice became animated as he shared some of this with me. He spoke of how Jehovah had formed the earth from disorganized matter, organizing it, bringing it light, and placing plants and animals on it.

During the telling, I settled once more into his arms, listening to his heart echo the beat of his words.

"After sharing this knowledge, he blessed me. Sarai, Jehovah blessed me." His voice was hushed with reverence.

"What did he bless you with?" I murmured, feeling the sacredness of his experience.

"He promised me a child from my loins to give me immense posterity, more than the number of stars in the heavens or grains of sand. He told me that our seed would be exiled to Egypt and become a considerable nation when they are finally freed after four hundred years."

"Freed? Pharaoh will enslave our children after all we have done for him?" I asked, vexation filling my voice. We had done so much for him. How could he think of such a thing?

"Not the Pharaoh we know, but one who does not know us or Jehovah. One who fears us. But all the land from Egypt to the Euphrates is ours."

"Will we have that many children to occupy all that land?" I leaned back to see his face.

"In time, Sarai. In time." He pulled me close to him again, and I lay quietly listening to his heartbeat and his breathing as it slowed into sleep.

"But my womb is dry. I cannot give you a child. How can we have this glorious blessing?" I asked in a murmur.

"Jehovah knows. Trust him," Abram murmured as he fell asleep.

I trusted Jehovah, but how could I give birth to a child? Jehovah must know of another way for Abram to have children. He had not given them to me.

I spent the night considering and fretting about the problem. How could I give Abram a child? I slipped from his arms and pulled a robe over my sleeping robe. I slipped through our tent door and stared into the night sky.

All the stars Abram had taught me about twinkled above me. Jehovah watched in his judgment seat somewhere up there.

"How am I to give Abram a child?" I cried softly so no one would hear my pleas but Jehovah. "My womb is dry. In the days of my youth, you did not fill it. What do I do now? How do I give Abram a child?"

The night sky was silent. So was Jehovah. This was my challenge, my problem to solve.

As the stars blinked out and the sky lightened, I returned to our bed. I still had no answer. Abram slept from exhaustion in trust.

There had to be a way. How could I lose Abram?

A light touch on my arm awakened me with a start. The sun still fought to rise above the mountains to the west.

"Mistress, the women wonder if we should wake the men to take the animals to pasture," Hagar asked in a low tone so she would not wake Abram.

"They celebrated late into the night. Let them sleep a bit longer. The animals will be fine if we let them wait."

"Yes, mistress," Hagar whispered.

She silently left our tent, but I heard her whispering to the women outside. "The mistress says the animals can wait. Our men celebrated late last night."

"Much too late," Bara said, not even attempting to keep her voice low. "They know the animals need to eat."

The women would not accept Hagar's answer nor move away from our tent. Shaking the sleep from my eyes, I dressed and joined the women outside. "The sun is barely up. Should the men not have another hour of sleep to honor their victory?"

"Perhaps they should," Bara said, "but the animals should not be required to wait to eat."

It was then I heard the plaintive bleating of the sheep and goats. I heaved a sigh. "Can we take the animals to pasture?"

"Us?" a woman cried, her eyes bulging.

I lifted a shoulder. "Why not? The animals are hungry."

"They do not know us as they know our men," Bara said, glancing around uneasily. "What do we do if the sheep run away from us? I have seen them do that with new herders."

My eyes roamed at each woman in the circle before I let my breath out heavily. "Perhaps you are right. We should waken our men."

"Or our boys who go with the men each day," a woman said, taking a step back.

"The sheep will listen to them no better than they will listen to us," I said. "It is time to wake our men. We should ensure they have a filling meal to soften their lack of sleep."

"They did it to themselves," Bara smirked. "I am happy to have Danil home, but it is time he returned to his responsibilities."

"So be it," I said and turned on my slippered heel to wake Abram.

"You would wake the master?" Hagar asked, following me with hesitant steps.

"I would. His sheep love him. They miss him as much as we did. Is our meal ready?"

She nodded. "I have grains cooking as always. I started them last night."

"Thank you, Hagar. I will go wake Abram."

She turned toward the cooking fires while I entered the tent. Abram lay on his side, watching the door as I entered.

"You thought you could take the sheep out to the pastures alone?" he asked.

I picked at a scratch on my hand. "I thought we could allow you more time to rest."

"The sheep would run."

"I know, now that I think of it. I saw them run when Shimon first tried to take them out alone." I giggled at the memory. "It would not have gone well for us."

"No," Abram said, smothering his laughter. "It would not. Thank Jehovah you decided to wake the men."

"I wanted good things for you," I said, staring at my feet. "Jehovah has promised so many important things to you."

Abram rose from the bed and whirled me in his arms. "Wonderful things for both of us. I can have none of these things without you."

"How?" I squeaked, but he had bounced into his clothing and did not hear.

I followed him slowly as he tromped through the tent and out to the cooking area. He lowered himself into the seat at the low table, waiting for his meal. Hagar handed him a bowl of cooked grains. He looked up at her with a smile.

Her return smile held a desire I had not noticed before. She gazed into his eyes with an intensity. Did he return it?

As she turned away, her face and arms had flushed red. She wanted my husband.

Abram is mine. You can find your own man. I am not sharing.

Then my focus shifted. Somehow, I saw them differently.

Hagar.

Hagar was the solution.

I can give her to Abram and she can bear us a child. Because she is my maid, the child will be mine as well.

My mouth went dry and I grinned at them. It seemed so right at that time. When I think back on that moment, I wonder how I could ever consider such a thing. But it seemed so right.

Abram needed a child. I could not give him one. Hagar was the solution.

I smoothed my face and joined them, accepting the grains Hagar gave me.

That night, we sat across from each other before going to bed. The words spilled from me. "Abram. Jehovah has promised you a child. You know I am past the time when I can bear you a child."

Abram coughed and lowered his brows, but I did not allow him to speak.

"I have the solution. You can take another woman to give you a child."

"But I am your husband."

"And Hagar is my handmaid." I blurted the words quickly so I could not change my mind. I stared into his eyes, not allowing him to break away. "If you take Hagar as your concubine, the child will be ours, and you will have the children promised by Jehovah."

"Sarai," Abram said, reaching out to touch my face. "Do you know what you are saying?"

"I cannot give you a child. We have tried all these years and Jehovah has not filled my belly with a child. My womb is dry. I no longer bleed as women bleed. How can I give you a child? The only way is for you to take another woman."

I inhaled and rushed on. "I know Hagar. She believes in Jehovah, so your child will learn of Him. You will have your child and your posterity. I would rather you take Hagar than go out into a city or among our followers to find another woman to take as a second wife."

Abram pinched the bridge of his nose and squeezed his eyes closed. "Jehovah can heal your womb."

"He has not in all these years. What makes you think He even wants to heal me? What makes you think He wants me to have a child? If He wanted me to have a child, we would have one already."

"Think about this, Sarai. Once I take her, we cannot go back. Do not be rash," he begged.

"I have thought about it all day. It is the only solution." My voice had lifted in pitch. I inhaled and lowered my voice. "This is the only answer."

Abram's jaw slackened and his eyes opened wide. He opened his mouth and shut it again.

I waited. I had said what needed to be said. Now it was up to him.

He rubbed his hand across his forehead. "Think about this ... No. Do not interrupt. Think about this tonight and tomorrow. If it still feels right to you, I will do it." He reached out and pulled me onto his lap. "I will do this only if you insist. I want no one but you. I want you to be the mother of my children, not Hagar, not any other woman."

I allowed the tension in me to release and fell into his arms. "I do not want to do this. I desire to be the mother of your children. I desire to be the mother of nations, as you will be the father of nations. Jehovah does not agree."

"I do not think you are correct in that decision."

"I am. Or I would have had children by now. Jehovah does not love me enough to give me a child." The tears I held back rushed down my face as I sobbed.

"I disagree. Jehovah loves you, and he has promised us a child. Trust Him. Think about this for more than tomorrow. I will not take Hagar until you are certain."

Chapter Seventeen

Answers

I spent much of the night tossing and turning. My mind would not relax and allow me to sleep. *Can I really give Abram to another woman? Can I listen to him with her?*

I would have to be kind and accepting. I was giving her to him. He was not taking her. Jehovah promised him many children from his body. Not from me. I was not able.

Finally, as the tent lightened with dawn's earliest light, I dozed off. When I woke, Abram had slipped from the bed and left the tent.

I dressed quickly and hurried out to see if he still ate his morning meal. But Abram had left with the herders. I would have to talk to him when he returned.

Later that afternoon, Hagar and I spun wool in the shade of the tent. Whenever we had spare time, we would spin to have enough to weave.

The day was hot, but a breeze helped keep us cool in the shade. I thought of the solution to our problem. How could I give Abram a child? We spoke of nothing important for nearly an hour, before words slipped out of my mouth unexpectedly.

"Jehovah spoke with Abram when he was gone. Jehovah promised him a vast posterity, greater than the number of the stars, more than the grains of sand."

"How will that happen?" Hagar asked. "You are past the time of childbirth."

"I know that," I said. "I have been given a solution."

She lifted her eyebrows, waiting for me to continue.

I sucked in a deep breath and spoke in a soft voice. "You are the answer. If you agree, I will give you to be Abram's concubine. You are still young. You need a child as much as I. Abram will give you a child for us, the three of us. I have seen you look at him. You love him."

"No, mistress." Hagar lifted her hands in front of her. "I do not love Abram as anything more than as my good master. I —"

"You need a man, and we need a child."

Hagar blew out her breath and the words she held within. "And you think I can give it to you?" She lifted her chin.

I swallowed twice before I could reply. "You are the only answer. Will you do it?"

"Will Abram have me? I will not do it if he does not want me." Hagar's voice was strained.

"We spoke of this last night. He loves me and believes it is possible for me to have a child, even in my old age. But good sense will prevail. He will accept this."

"If he does not, I will forget you ever suggested it."

You will never forget the suggestion. You are a woman. I will never forget. But I will do this. Abram needs a child. I cannot give him that child. Sorrow filled my heart. I wanted to be the one.

When Abram returned from the meadows with the sheep, I waited for him. I wanted to pounce on him like the lions he protected the sheep from, but waited until after we ate. Then I led him from the camp, requesting he take me for a walk.

When we were away from everyone, I spoke. "I talked to Hagar today."

"You what?" his voice was low and careful. "I thought we agreed you would wait."

"I spent the night thinking about it, as you suggested. While we worked together spinning, the words popped out. I told her you need a child, and she can give it to us."

"She can, but so can you."

I laughed a short, bitter laugh. "I am past my time for bearing children. Hagar is not. I give her to you."

"You must announce it publicly. Can you do that?"

I swallowed the sudden fullness in my throat three times before I could speak. "When?"

"I will not allow this to happen for a week. You must be certain."

"I am. You need a child."

"I can wait a week for you to be certain." Abram gathered me into his arms and held me close.

"Do one thing for me, please," I begged.

"Anything for you, my love."

"Move Hagar's tent to the other side of the camp. I cannot bear the thought of listening to you together."

"I will not do that to you. We will move her tent after you make the announcement. But she will still be your handmaid. You will need her close enough to assist you."

"Then, make a makeshift tent and take her out to it for a month. I can live without her for that long."

"No. I will not leave you for that long. We will be discreet. You need not hear us or know we are together."

Tears leapt to my eyes. "Thank you, but I will know."

He stroked my hair. "You will not hear us." His voice cracked. "I will keep it private. I love you too much to hurt you. I do not want to do this. Please change your mind."

"You know I cannot. You must have a child for your blessing to be valid. What else can I do?" My tears wet his shoulder.

"You can wait for Jehovah. He can do anything," Abram pled, his voice breaking with his tears.

"We have waited on Jehovah for more than fifty years. My body is too old. Take Hagar. Her womb is young and seeking a child."

"After you decide to announce it. But not for at least a week."

We spent much of the next week together. Abram stayed with me when the herders took the animals out to graze. He held my hand and treated me like a new bride. His gentle touch was bittersweet. I knew he would leave me for her as soon as I announced to the camp that I gave Hagar to him.

Thinking about it made my stomach turn. How could I give my beloved Abram to another woman, even Hagar, my handmaid? I fought off the tears, not wanting Abram to see them.

However, at night, when he slept, my tears watered my pillow. How could I do it?

Two Sabbaths later, I rose at the end of our worship service. "I stand to make an announcement."

Abram stared at me. I suspect he hoped I had changed my mind.

"I am old. You know we have no children. Abram deserves a child as an heir." I glanced at Eliezer. "You will receive an inheritance from us, but Abram needs a child of his body. For this reason, I give my handmaiden, Hagar, to him."

I gestured for Hagar to come forward, then turned and took Abram's hand and set her hand in his.

"Any child of yours will be a child of ours. May you bring us posterity."

I stepped away and sat down.

"Are you willing to accept me?" Abram asked Hagar.

"I will," Hagar said. Her eyes shone like I had never seen before. "And will you take me?"

My heart crumpled, but I would not retract my words. They were spoken. Abram needed a child and I could not be the one to give him one.

"I will."

Abram and Hagar walked out of the tent we used for these meetings. The tent buzzed. I stood and left, brushing off Bara and all the others who wanted to reach out to me. I could not bear to talk about it. Not now.

I went to our tent and lay on our bed with the pillow over my ears. I spent the next hours sobbing my frustration to Jehovah. Why had he not allowed a child to fill my womb? I had always wanted a child. *If nothing is impossible for you, why has a child not filled my womb?*

Before night, my tears dried. I felt a warmth in my heart. I had done the right thing, although it tore me to shreds. Abram needed a child. I sacrificed my selfish desires for my husband to Jehovah.

I washed my face and left the tent. At the cooking fire, I stirred the coals, set a pot of water over them, and started a stew. I needed food, and Abram and Hagar would need food eventually.

I ate, then pulled the stew to the side of the fire. They could eat when they were ready.

Each night I slept clutching Abram's pillow, wishing he were with me, wanting him beside me. In Egypt, we hoped to be together again. Only Pharaoh came between us, and Jehovah protected me from him. A hollow ache filled my soul. This was my doing. I hated every minute, knowing he was with another woman, wanting him to be with me. But Abram needed a child, and I could not provide him with one.

Did Hagar know how much I had sacrificed to allow her to mother his child?

Each morning I washed the tears from my face and went out into the camp as usual, visiting with the women, caring for the ill, checking on the lonely. All the time I wished one would see my sorrow, care for me in my loneliness, even as I brushed away all kindness from the other women. I wanted Abram to care for me, not another woman.

I interpreted the looks many women gave me as comfort in my grief. I told any who asked I was happy to do it for Abram. I was happy for him. However, I grieved for myself.

Chapter Eighteen

Concubine

Six mornings later, Abram entered our tent with Hagar's fragrance on him. I struggled not to retch.

When he held his arms out to me, I shook my head. "I cannot come to your arms with her smell on you."

He left the tent with clean clothes, returning after he bathed. Then I fell into his arms and sobbed.

He soothed me with soft words, running his hands through my hair and down my back. I so missed his touch.

"Is it over?" I asked.

"How can it be? You gave her to me. I am responsible for her now as a concubine. She deserves some of my time and attention, as you do. I must now share myself with her."

I bit the inside of my mouth and fought to keep my face still. "I did not know. I thought it would only be a matter of giving her a child ..."

He stepped back to look into my face. "I must now treat her as a wife. Did you not understand?"

"I did not want to understand."

"This is difficult for me, as it is for you. But the decision has been made, and we are joined now, the three of us."

"I will bear it if she gives you a child." I stepped back into his arms and kissed him.

Desire filled his kisses. How could he desire me after being with Hagar, a young woman? But he did.

After that, our lives changed.

Although Hagar continued to be my maidservant, cooking for us and helping me with the cleaning and other chores, she held herself differently. I found her looking at me with haughty eyes.

I could prove nothing and ignored it. She could not drive me from my beloved Abram.

Over time, Hagar's haughty looks became snide, and I heard hateful comments under her breath.

"I am more of a woman than you."

"Your husband sleeps with me more than he sleeps with you."

"Abram loves me more than he loves you."

It tore my soul into shreds to hear such words, for I feared she spoke the truth. Did he love her more than me? Was she more of a woman than me?

He lay with her frequently. Did it show he loved her more?

"I carry the child you could never have."

She did. I saw it before she spoke the words. As with Senet, I saw her body glow. It was why I gave her to Abram, but her pride in it hurt me.

"She despises me," I cried to Abram one night. "She taunts me, saying you love her more than you do me."

"You know I do not. I only go to her because you sent me."

His calm voice infuriated me. Could he not see my side of it?

"Will you speak to her?" Jealousy filled me. Hot burning filled my stomach from the desire to scratch her eyes out. I hated it.

Abram pulled me onto his lap. "She is your handmaid. She is yours to chastise. Do as you please with her."

"You would not mind?"

"I trust you to chastise her, within reason. You are a daughter of Jehovah. Hagar is your maidservant."

He held me for many long minutes until the dragon of jealousy retreated.

Yet, the next day, Hagar continued her spiteful ways. As we worked together spinning, her words flowed across me, cutting me.

"I carry the child you never could," she crowed.

"And I gave you my husband for that child," I cried. "Abram is my husband. He loves me and will always love me. If you do not stop your hateful whispering, he will never lay with you again."

Hagar laughed. "He loves me more than you. He will soon spend all his nights in my bed, not yours."

I did not understand what happened next. I had never lost control like that before, nor since. But I lifted my spindle and swung at her. I hit her in the face and she cried out.

I should have stopped then, but the dragon of jealousy overcame me and I hit her again and again. She hid her face, trying to avoid my spindle.

At last, she could take no more, and ran from me out of the camp into the wilderness. I glowered after her for many long breaths. Then it hit me.

"What have I done?" I cried, falling heavily into my chair. "She is gone. What will Abram do for a child? *What will he do to me for driving her away? What will he say to me?*"

I blankly rocked back and forth in my chair, waiting for Abram's rebuke. What would he say? Did he know Hagar carried his child?

When Abram returned, he plopped in his chair next to mine. "Where is Hagar? Should she not have dinner nearly prepared?"

I lifted my tear-stained face to him. "I do not know what happened. We were spinning. She taunted me. She said she carried the child I would never carry and that you loved her more than me." I clutched my arms to my chest and hunched my shoulders closer to my ears. "She said you planned to spend all your nights in her bed." I clenched my fists and stood up to pace. "My spindle was in her face before I knew what I did." I turned away from him. "I did not intend to hit her."

Abram joined me and encircled me in his arms. "Where is she now?"

I burst into tears. "I do not ... I do not know. She ran from me." I fought to breathe through the pain in the back of my throat. "I chased her away."

"Sarai," he crooned. "You are my first and only love. I will never love her more than you. You are my first and beloved wife."

"What will you do? Will you search for her?" I said through gasping tears.

"What do you think I should do?" His voice calmed me as he brushed his hand through my hair.

"Will she return?" I asked.

I felt him shrug. "Hagar is a proud woman. She may return, but she would not want me to send men looking for her."

"Will you go?"

"If she does not return by morning." Abram stepped back a half step and gazed into my eyes. "She is strong. Let her decide what she should do. If she does not come back by tomorrow, I will send someone out to search for her."

"You are not angry? She carries your child," I asked.

"Yes, she told me. Her pride will take her a distance, but when she has no water, she will return."

"That is not safe for the child," I said with a gasp.

"No, but Hagar must learn a lesson and she will only learn it when she struggles."

"I have caused her to struggle." I bit my lip. "I must repent of my anger. I should not have allowed her to push me so far into the jealousy dragon."

"Apologize to her when she returns. I believe she will return."

That night, a storm blew through the camp. I worried about Hagar. How would she survive a storm in the desert?

I climbed out of bed and knelt on the floor where I begged Jehovah to protect Hagar. I poured out my grief for my behavior, my sorrow that she fled from me. I prayed for the unborn babe within her.

At some point, Abram joined me, praying with me for her and the child. The furious wind raged outside our tent.

"How can Hagar survive this storm?" I cried.

"I do not know. She must need to learn to depend on Jehovah." He took my hand as he prayed, concentrating on Hagar and her child in the wind.

Eventually, the gale slowed, but Abram could not leave. So much dust filled the air he could not see or breathe.

"How is Hagar surviving this?" I asked.

"If she is, it is only because Jehovah is blessing her."

I hunched in our tent waiting for the dust in the air to settle, words of prayer filling my head and heart.

The sun finally rose, shining weakly through the dust in the air. I found cold food for us to eat inside while we waited for the dust to settle.

"I will tie a cloth over my face and search for Hagar when the dust settles a bit more. With this much, I would pass by her and never see her."

Helplessness filled me. I could not go out to search for her. Would she even accept help from me? A sob escaped from the pit of my stomach. Abram touched me, consoling me.

Later, Abram pulled a scarf over his nose and throat and ran out to check on the animals. They had bedded down close together and buried their faces in their own fur or the body of another. All were safe.

When he returned with the news, he paced back and forth inside the tent, mumbling to himself. I stooped with my head bowed, praying.

Abram pulled the scarf back across his nose and mouth and left the tent. All I could do was stand and watch him leave.

My stomach roiled as I imagined everything that could have happened to Hagar. Then fear clutched at my throat as I considered the challenges Abram faced as he searched for her. How would he find her? The wind would have blown away her tracks. Did he have enough water for himself and her? Fears whirled in my mind.

The hours passed slowly. I could no longer pace from one wall to another. I picked up my spindle and spun the wool into thread.

After a time, I stared down at the spindle in my hand. I had used this to drive away the woman I gave to Abram, the woman who had been my maid and helper. How could a follower of Jehovah do such a thing?

I fell to my knees. "Forgive me, Jehovah. Bring Abram and Hagar back, so I may beg her forgiveness as well."

Late that afternoon, as I walked to the well for water, I saw Abram carrying Hagar through the camp. I ran to them.

"Does she live?" I asked.

"She does," Abram said. "I found her staggering toward the camp, mumbling something about an Ishmael."

"What or who is Ishmael?" I asked, trotting beside him as he carried her to her tent.

"I do not know. Perhaps God heard her cries."

I pulled the tent door back so he could duck under it with her. He laid her gently on her bed and brushed the sand-filled hair from her face.

"She will want a bath when she wakes," I said. "But for now, I will brush the sand from her hair."

I searched her table in front of her mirror until I found her brush. Then I perched beside her on a stool, brushing the sand from her hair as she had brushed my hair when we first met. Abram left the tent in search of something.

"That feels wonderful," she mumbled.

"You are awake," I cried. "I have feared for you since you ran away from me."

Hagar moaned. "I was wrong to taunt you. Jehovah sent an angel to me in the midst of the storm. He told me to return and submit myself to you."

"Are you injured?" I asked, brushing the last of the tangles and dirt from her hair.

"Bruised from my falls and sore from the sand blowing into my skin, but no, I am not injured."

"When you are ready, I will bring you hot bath water."

"You are my mistress. I should bring you bath water," Hagar argued.

"Tomorrow you may. Today, allow me to bring you water. I beg you to forgive my cruelty. I should never have hit you."

Hagar sat up in her bed. "And I should not have taunted you and caused you such pain. I forgive you if you will forgive me."

I shook my head quickly. "You are forgiven."

The tent door opened and Abram peered in. "Are you covered?"

At Hagar's nod, Abram opened the tent door wider and stepped back. A man brought in a tub. Others followed with buckets of hot water. When they filled the tub, they backed out of the tent.

"You can have that bath you need," Abram said. "When you are clean and able to talk, please come talk with us."

Hagar nodded. Abram beckoned to me to follow him.

"Can you do this alone?" I asked.

"I am able. Go with Abram." She rose slowly, dropped her clothing, and stepped into the tub.

I left her tent and walked to ours with Abram in silence. When he settled in his chair, he pulled me to his lap.

"Sarai, my love," he murmured. "I love you more than life itself. I go to Hagar because you gave her to me as a wife. I care for her only in that way. She will never take your place. Dampen your dragon of jealousy. I will never stop loving you."

He pulled me close and held me as I clung to him with weak muscles.

At last, I moved to the chair beside him. "Hagar will finish her bath and come to talk with us. She does not need to see us so close."

He scooted his chair next to mine. "But she needs to know we are still close."

A scratch on our tent door warned us someone wanted to enter.

"Come," Abram called.

Hagar entered looking lovely with her hair flowing loosely over her shoulders, rather than tied back in a braid. She fell to her knees in front of us. "I come to beg your forgiveness for all the trouble I have caused you. And to thank you for rescuing me. I do not know if I could have returned to your tent without your help."

Abram nodded and took her hand. "I forgive you. You are part of our family. I could not let you struggle alone in the wilderness."

Hagar turned to me. "I grieve for the heartache I caused you. Please forgive me for the harsh words I spoke to you."

I lifted her from her knees. "I told you many years ago I would stand by your side as long as you are faithful to me."

She stepped into my arms and squeezed me tight. "I will never forget that. I will remain faithful to you."

Over the next hours, Hagar reclined in a chair across from us and shared with us what had happened when she ran into the wilderness.

"I ran away from you and your spindle without thinking. I took nothing with me. I ran and ran until I could run no farther."

I ducked my head at these words as my face warmed.

"Then the wind increased, blowing sand in every direction. I thought I should return to you. But I did not know where home and you were. I was lost." She swallowed and rubbed her forehead.

"I pulled my scarf across my face and stumbled onward. My heart hurt and my stomach clenched. How would I find home again?"

"How frightening," I said, my throat tightening.

"It was. At last, I collapsed to the ground, no longer able to move forward. I pulled my scarf over my head and curled into a ball, hoping the wind would drop and I would find my way home once more."

Abram nodded. "That is always the right thing to do when you have lost your way."

"I must have slept. Eventually, the wind calmed, but dirt and sand filled the air. The wind had dried me out and I had been without water since before I left. I longed for water."

"How did you survive without water?" I asked.

"When the dust cleared, I discovered I had stopped by a fountain of water. I crawled toward it. When a man offered me a cup of water, I took it and drank thirstily."

"You should not drink so fast or you will be sick," Abram murmured.

"The man by the water said the same thing. I slowed my drinking to a sip and drank three more cups of water."

"Who was the man? A wandering stranger?" I asked.

"I asked the same thing," Hagar said. "'I come as a messenger from Jehovah,' he said."

"An angel from Jehovah," Abram said with a decisive nod.

"He asked me how I got there in the middle of the wilderness in a sandstorm, and where did I plan to go?"

I rolled my lips inward, knowing I had caused her trouble.

"I told him I fled from the face of my mistress, Sarai, for I had spoken ungracious words and she dealt harshly with me. I half expected the messenger, the angel, to tell me I had done the right thing and direct me onward to a safe place. But he did not. Instead, he told me to return to my mistress and submit to her hand." Hagar dropped her head. "He was right. I was wrong to be so spiteful."

"Did the angel tell you more?" Abram asked. "I have found when an angel comes, there is more to their message."

"He did. He promised my children would multiply so greatly I could not number them all."

Abram glanced at me with a look of understanding. He had received the same promise.

"He told me I am with child, which I knew," Hagar continued, looking inward and remembering, unaware of our communication. "I shall bear a son and his name is to be Ishmael, because Jehovah has heard my complaints in my affliction."

"Anything else?" Abram asked.

"He shall be as a wild ass, loving freedom and wandering the desert."

"You and your child will be blessed," I said.

"You will," Abram added.

"When the angel left me, I knelt beside the water and considered his words. I had been unkind and thoughtless. I promise I will not continue this. I have changed. You can trust me to be faithful to you. I will never again think of myself as better than you."

Abram pulled Hagar into a hug. "We feared for your safety while you were gone."

"You feared for your child," Hagar whispered.

"Yes, Hagar, I feared for Ishmael, though I did not know his name. But I also feared for his mother. We are grateful you found your way home."

She returned his embrace. "Thank you for finding me. I would not have found my way home alone."

I joined them and put my arms around them both. "I love you both. Please accept my apology."

Abram kissed my forehead, then kissed Hagar's forehead. We were a family at last.

Chapter Nineteen

New Names

For the next few months, I spent time with Hagar, working together to prepare for Ishmael's birth. We spun and wove blankets and soft fabric, which we used to make clothing for the babe. I joined Hagar cooking and cleaning and doing all I could to help.

One morning Hagar did not join me at the cooking fire. I checked the grains set beside the fire the night before, then rushed to her tent to investigate her disappearance. She lay in her bed, writhing in pain.

My heart leapt within me. What caused such pain?

"Hagar," I cried. "What is happening? Is your baby well?"

"My stomach is cramping," she said, rolling back and forth in her bed.

"Is it time for the child to come?" I caught her hand and squeezed it.

"I do not know," she wailed.

"I will go get Bara. She will know. She has brought many children into this world." I lifted Hagar's fingers from my hands. "I will return soon."

"But what ... about ... the morning ... meal?" she asked between breaths.

"It is cooking. I will get Bara. She will know what to do for you." I slipped from her tent and rushed toward Bara's tent.

I found her outside, standing over her cooking fire. "Sarai, I did not expect to see you this early in the morning."

"Hagar is cramping and rolling in pain in her bed!"

"Is it her time?" Bara looked up from pouring grains into her pot.

I nodded. "She is writhing in pain. I told her I would get you to help. I have never helped with the birthing of a child."

Bara quickly calculated the time since I gave Hagar to Abram. "It is her time. I will be there as soon as I get my supplies. Let her know." Bara turned on her heel and entered her tent. I heard her call for a granddaughter to come cook the meal.

I sprinted back to Hagar's tent. "Bara is coming. She is gathering her supplies."

Hagar grabbed my hand. "Thank you, Sarai. Stay with me. I am fearful. I saw mothers die in Egypt during birth."

"You will not die. Bara will be here to help you," I murmured gently, brushing her damp hair from her forehead.

"You think I will not die?" Hagar moaned.

"No. The angel promised you a healthy son. You will live to help him grow. I have heard that birth is difficult." My hand hurt from her grip, but I did not remove it from hers.

"Stay with me, Sarai," Hagar begged.

Bara bustled into the tent. "What is happening here? Has your little one decided it is time to be born?"

"It seems so," I said. "Hagar. I need to go take the grains off the fire."

"Come back," she begged.

"I will."

I hurried from Hagar's tent to our cooking fire and pulled the grains to the edge.

"Where is Hagar?" Abram asked as he settled into his chair.

"It is her time."

"Time?" His face twisted in confusion.

"Ishmael is coming. Can you dish up your own food? Hagar wants me to be with her."

"Yes. Go."

I turned and fled back to Hagar's tent. I could hear her moan before I reached it. It must hurt.

I had never gone in when a woman gave birth, never invited, never given birth to my own child, and did not know what to expect, except pain. A lot of pain. From the stories told by other women, I knew it would hurt, probably more than the pain when I lost my one child. *But that pain never ends. Hagar's pain will end with the joy of a child.*

As I entered the tent, Hagar screamed my name. I rushed to her side and took her hand.

"I am here," I whispered.

"Sarai, why did you not tell me it hurts this bad?"

"I did not know. I have never experienced giving birth. Did you not ask Bara and the other mothers here?"

Hagar trembled from head to toe. "I spoke with them. I did not understand."

"I am here to help with your pain. Hold my hand when it hurts. I can take some of it from you," I said, clasping her hand.

Her face contorted with a scream. I clasped her hand and murmured soft words to her.

The pain eased and she trembled all over.

Bara stood at her feet. "You are doing well. Scream if you must. It helps push the child out of you."

Hagar squeezed her eyes shut and nodded.

"You are doing well," I repeated. "Bara says it will not be long." I looked at Bara to see if I was correct.

"Not if her pains come as hard as that last one. Here comes another. It will not be long indeed."

Hagar clutched my hand until I feared it would never lie flat again, but I did not pull it back. I held on to her hand and spoke words of love into her ears.

The sun had not moved to its apex when I pushed the tent door open to find Abram. He waited next to the tent door.

"Your son is here," I said. "Come in and see him."

Bara had cleaned the boy and wrapped him in a blanket we had woven for him and placed him in Hagar's arms. She gathered the mess of the afterbirth into a rag and carried it out when Abram entered.

"You have a beautiful son," she said as she passed him.

Abram's eyes were on Hagar. He had heard her pain, had felt the agony, as I had. Ishmael lay at her breast, suckling. Love filled his eyes. He had a son. And Hagar had borne him.

Jealousy struggled to overwhelm me, but I fought it down. This was our child, theirs and mine. I had desired this for Abram and Jehovah had given Ishmael to him.

"Do you want to hold him?" Hagar asked.

"May I?" Abram crept closer to them.

"Sit," I said, pointing to the stool near Hagar. "I will put him in your arms."

While Abram sat, I carefully lifted the tiny boy and embraced him before setting him in his father's arms. I positioned myself behind him so I could look over his shoulder into the babe's face.

His tiny face peered up at his father. Tiny lips. Big brown eyes. I could see Abram in him. I swallowed the bile of jealousy once more and smiled at Hagar.

"He is red and hairy," Abram said.

"All babies are red and hairy," Bara said, returning to the tent. "That will change. I am here to finish cleaning Hagar, then I will leave you alone to be a family."

She finished washing Hagar and pulled the blanket over her, then she patted Hagar's legs. "You did well."

Bara slipped out of the tent.

"Family," Hagar whispered. "I did not think I would hear that word including me again."

I did not plan for our family to grow like this when I was young. But here we were. Growing with Hagar and Ishmael.

Abram settled Ishmael in one arm, then reached out to smooth Hagar's hair away from her face. "You are part of our family. You and Ishmael."

We stayed with her day and night for the next week, helping her to care for the child as she healed from her travail. Abram slept next to Hagar, and I slept on a mat on the floor next to the bed.

Things had changed since the days Hagar slept close to me to care for me.

Ishmael grew strong over the years, tagging after his father as soon as he could walk. Abram often lifted him to his shoulders and carried him to feed the sheep.

I would stand with Hagar to watch them together. My admiration and pride in him almost matched hers.

Ishmael called me Auntie Sarai as soon as he could speak. He made me happy. Jehovah had blessed Abram with the child He had promised.

Then, in Ishmael's thirteenth year, Abram came to me trembling with an ashen face.

"I have walked with Jehovah today."

I allowed a small gasp to escape. I was blessed to hear from Jehovah through Abram. Sometimes, though, I thought it would be nice to hear his voice for myself. "What did Jehovah tell you today?"

"He made a covenant with me and all my family, all my children, which he promises to multiply. And my children will be known among nations. And from Ishmael, many."

"We knew that. He promised the same things before."

"Yes, but this time, He promised more, gave more, and expects more."

I lifted my chin as a tightness filled my stomach. "What more did He promise? What did He give? And what more can He expect?"

How could Jehovah expect more of me? I gave my husband to another.

"Jehovah changed my name to Abraham, no longer to be called Abram, because I am a father of many nations."

I spoke his new name. "A-bra-ham. Similar but different."

"Yes, and he gave you a new name as well."

"Me? What name shall I be called at this old age?"

"You are to be called Sarah, for you will be a mother of nations. Many kings shall come from you."

I laughed. "Me? A mother of nations? That is Hagar. Did she receive a new name as well?" *How many times have I heard this promise? And still, nothing.*

"No. She did not, and no. It is not Hagar, and she did not receive a new name. I also laughed. How can I, at nearly a hundred years old, father a child, and you, past the time to give birth in your nineties, give birth to a child? I begged Jehovah for Ishmael to follow Him."

I shook my head. "I am dry. No child comes from me, but I accept the title."

"No. Jehovah promised that you, Sarah, my beloved wife, will bear a son who we are to name Isaac. The covenant made between Jehovah and me will come through him and his many children."

"I am old and dry. The covenant will come through Ishmael."

"No, Sarah." He used my new name again. It sounded different, but right. "Ishmael will be fruitful and receive twelve sons and they will become a vast nation. But the covenant is with Isaac, who will be born to you. He will be born to you, Sarah, within the year."

I opened and closed my mouth three times before I could reply. At last, words slipped past my lips. "Marvelous promises indeed. Wonderful gifts in our new names. But what does Jehovah expect? It must be extraordinary for you to come to me white and shuddering."

"It is. I am commanded to take upon me an outward covenant. I and all the males among us are to circumcise the flesh of our foreskin as a symbol of the covenant between us and Jehovah. He will be our God and we will be his people. It will be an everlasting covenant between Jehovah and us and all our followers and all our family."

My heart pounded and my fingers became icy. "All your …?"

He nodded.

"When will you do this?"

"Today. If a man cannot accept it, I will send him from among us, for it is a covenant with our God."

"What can I do?" I asked, hoping I would not be called on to perform this covenant for them.

"Take the women to the other side of the camp and explain the covenant to them. Their men will need them after the circumcision. Help prepare them for it while I share with the men."

I went through the camp, walking from tent to tent, calling the women to join me. When all of us had come together, I shared with them the thing that had to be done.

"You will need to comfort and help heal your men. Dara, can you tell us what will be required?"

Dara closed her eyes in thought, then spoke of possible bandaging and healing remedies.

"They will be in pain. I suggest we give them broth and bread tonight, perhaps even tomorrow. They will need the food to heal, but their stomachs will take little after such a shock."

The women murmured to each other, discussing types of bandages and healing remedies.

I spoke once more. "We must also consider another challenge. We will have no men to protect us until they heal. We must stand guard at the passes. Who can do this?"

They stared at their feet and all everywhere else, anywhere but at me.

Hagar lifted a hand. "I have no practice with a sword, but I have gone to the meadows with Ishmael. I can carry a shepherd's crook. It will stop a man if I hit him with it, even as weak as I am."

Yael lifted her hand. "I had not thought of using a shepherd's staff. I can use my Benayah's staff. The curve at the end will pull a man off his feet."

Adi lifted her eyes to mine. "I have used my Shemaya's crook to guide my sons. I can stand guard if I am with another. I fear I am not strong enough to do it alone."

The women lifted their heads. The fear left their eyes and animation filled their voices. We soon had assignments made, with daughters taking early times in the rotation and older women filling in.

When we had settled the watch times, we hurried to our homes to prepare broth, healing ointments, and bandages.

From the other side of the camp, I heard the roar of the men. Abraham must have shared the covenant with them. Their voices soon quieted.

Later, Abraham told me he had Danil circumcise him first, slathering an ointment on him. Then, he circumcised Ishmael, and all the rest of the men in the camp.

He and Ishmael limped home, leaning on each other. Hagar took her son into her tent to tend to his injury. I cared for Abraham.

My Abraham. And I was no longer Sarai, but Sarah.

Jehovah blessed us in the week that followed. Although we set women as guards in the passes surrounding our valley, no one came to take advantage of our weakness.

Our men healed quickly and soon took the sheep back to the hills and meadows to feed.

About two weeks after the men stood guard once more, I worked inside weaving one evening while Abraham reclined in our tent door one hot afternoon. He leapt from the door and ran out toward the path in front of our tent.

I shrugged, and continued to weave, as he had run to meet herders before, until he hurried into the tent.

"Sarah," he cried. "We have special visitors. Quickly make three fine cakes for them."

Before I could ask questions, he was gone. I heard him calling to a young herder, telling him to dress and cook a young calf. These visitors must be special.

They rested just outside our tent door in the shade of a cedar tree, visiting with Abraham.

I made the cakes and took them out to the visitors, who smiled up at me. Their beautiful blue eyes filled me with love, overwhelming me. I could understand why Abraham wanted to give them the best he had and keep them here to visit. I nodded and returned to the tent, although I perched behind the door rather than returning to my weaving.

After the men ate the calf, I heard one visitor say, "Where is your wife, Sarah?"

I shrunk behind the tent door, but I wanted to hear what they had to say.

Abraham answered, "She is in the tent."

The visitors rose to leave. One said, "I will return in the time it takes for a life to grow in a womb. In that time, Sarah, thy wife, shall have a son."

Me! A son! I am old and past the time of having children. I laughed inside. *Shall we have pleasure like that together again, since Abraham is old like me? It cannot be.*

The visitor lifted his voice to be sure I could hear. "Why does Sarah laugh and say she is old? Is anything too difficult for Jehovah? Trust in Him. All things are possible. I shall return and Sarah shall have a son."

I stepped out of the tent with trembling lips. "I did not laugh. I know all things are possible."

"No," the visitor said. "You laughed. See what Jehovah can do, even to a dry womb like yours."

Abraham escorted the visitors down the road a distance.

"How can it be so?" I asked Abraham when he finally returned to the tent.

"All is possible with Jehovah. We must trust him." He took me into his arms and held me close.

"I fear for Lot," he said. "The angels now travel to Sodom and Gomorrah. I stood with them as they left, and the leader told me of their next mission."

"What will they do that causes you to fear?" I asked, trembling like a young woman in his arms as he ran his hands through my hair.

"They will destroy those cities if they do not find ten righteous men there. First, he said he would not destroy them for fifty, and I asked him if he would destroy them if they lacked but five men."

My jaw dropped. "You argued with an angel?"

"I tried to save those people. When he agreed to forty-five, I asked if He would save them if there were forty, then twenty. At last, he agreed to ten. I pray there are ten righteous men in Sodom and Gomorrah."

"Lot, his sons-in-law, and ... That is three. Surely there will be seven more in those two big cities."

"I pray there are," Abraham said. He took me in his arms and carried me to our bed. "We must prove Jehovah right. We must do our part to have a son."

"I am willing," I giggled. "My womb may be dry, but I enjoy being with you."

We spent time together, loving one another in ways we had not since we were newly married. Hope sprouted in my soul.

Chapter Twenty

Blessing

Each morning after that, Abraham rose early and went to the hills where he could see the plains where Sodom and Gomorrah lay. On the third day when he returned, his hair had lost its gloss and hung limply to his shoulders. In his previously dark hair, strands of white streaked through.

"What has happened?" I asked.

He swayed as I helped him to a chair. He rubbed his eyes and stared out to the east.

What has happened to my beloved Abraham? And what about Lot and Galya? Are they safe? He feared for them.

At last, he tried to speak, but the words jumbled in his mouth. I handed him a cup of wine and he took a small sip.

When he swallowed, he could speak again. "I stood on the hill looking toward the east, thinking of Lot."

"What has happened? Are they safe?"

"Per-perhaps," he stuttered. "I looked toward Sodom and Gomorrah where he lives, and ..." he rolled his lips inward, then coughed.

"Are Lot and Galya safe?"

"I do not know. Huge pillars of smoke rose from the plain. A hot, fiery smoke, as if from a furnace. I fear for Lot and his family."

I took his hand and together we wept until he slid to his knees.

"We must pray for their safety," he said.

I knelt and joined his prayers, begging Jehovah to protect our family.

Abraham sent a messenger toward the conflagration, asking them to discover if Lot still lived.

Abraham and I climbed the hill often in the next week, watching the flames diminish. Smoke flowed across our sky. Something bad had happened. We prayed for Lot, Galya, and their family.

Before the messenger returned with news, Abraham and Danil determined we must move southward again to find a greener place for our animals to graze.

We found pastureland in Gerar, between Kadesh and Shur, where we set up our tents.

Unfortunately, Abimelech, the king of Gerar, heard about us. He had heard of my beauty, and desired me, even in my old age. He had other wives, but none could conceive a child. He believed if he took me as a wife, they would have children.

Once again, Abraham asked me to tell Abimelech I was his sister, for this time, Abimelech would certainly kill him to have access to me. It had been a month since our visitors. I felt changes within me. But I had not told Abraham yet. Things had been busy as we moved. Abraham worried about Lot, Galya, and their children. Now, Abimelech wanted me.

And I would be required to say I was Abraham's sister.

I cried to Abraham. "You promised this would never happen again." I faced him with arms folded tightly across my chest.

"What can I do? Abimelech desires you for his wife. He will kill me if you say I am your husband." Tears ran down his face.

Tears fell across my face and dress for a time as I wildly considered the choices we had. "Trust Jehovah?" I asked.

"We must," he agreed. He took me into his arms and we wept together.

Abimelech sent a messenger to our camp who took me away from Abraham and to his palace.

Once again, I entered women's quarters as a hostage for Abraham, praying to Jehovah to protect my child and me. "You gave me this child, Jehovah," I prayed. "Please keep him and me safe."

Once again, women bathed me and washed my hair in fragrant soaps. They took me to a room where they dressed me in a soft, sheer dress, then introduced me to the women of the women's quarter. There, the women offered me kindness that the women of Memphis had not given me.

Sadiqe called me to sit next to her and honored me with sweet cakes and morsels of meat. Each night, when Abimelech entered our quarters, she enticed him to her bed, and the tension in my body released unexpectedly.

This happened for two weeks. Then, my stomach betrayed me. I could no longer keep food down. The mess horrified me. I, an old woman, could not control my stomach. It happened again, in front of Sadiqe.

"You are with child?" Sadiqe chastised as she handed me a cup of cool water. "None of our women can carry a child."

I wiped away the smelly slime from my lips and gratefully accepted the water. "Who would have thought an old woman like me, one whose womb had been dry for years, would now accept a child?"

"It is a miracle," one of Sadiqe's maids cried.

"It is a miracle. Jehovah has blessed me."

I reflected on the day the messengers came to promise me, a barren old woman, a child. I had laughed that day. I could not laugh when my stomach rebelled. I would have a child.

The next day, Abimelech sent for Abraham. When he arrived, he sent to the women's quarters for me. Sadiqe escorted me into his audience room. Excitement filled me when I learned my beloved was so close. I desperately missed him.

"What have you done to us?" Abimelech asked. "What have I done to offend you that you would cause such a tremendous curse to fall on my house?"

"What do you mean?" Abraham asked, glancing around the room, then catching my eyes with his.

"God came to me in a dream last night," Abimelech said, pacing in front of Abraham. "He called me a dead man because I took a woman who is another man's wife."

I swallowed deeply. Jehovah had heard my prayers.

"I fell on my face and begged God to spare me and my people," Abimelech continued. "I told him I had not come near your wife. Would God slay a righteous nation? I reminded Him you had told me Sarah is your sister, and even Sarah had said you were her brother. I am innocent."

Abraham fell to his knees to beg forgiveness, but Abimelech lifted him up. "God told me I am innocent, as long as I do not touch your woman and had not sinned with her. He warned me to restore her to you, for you are a prophet who will pray for me and my household. But if I did not return your wife, I and all my household would die."

Abimelech strode to me and took me by the arm and led me to Abraham. "Here is your wife. Take her."

Abraham's arm encircled me.

"Why would you put me and my household in such danger?" Abimelech demanded. "Why did you say Sarah is your sister?"

Abraham bowed his head. "I did not know you feared God and thought you would kill me to take my wife from me." He swallowed twice before continuing. "Sarah is my sister, for she is the daughter of my father, but not the daughter of my mother. In our youth, she became my wife."

I tried to step back. I had not known this. A tightness filled my chest and I breathed slowly to contain it. *My father was not Terah.* But Abraham held me close, keeping me from leaving his side. "Many years ago, I asked Sarah to tell the kings of the nations we enter I am her brother, that they would not slay me."

I glanced into his eyes, and he gently shook his head. I would learn more when we returned to our tent.

Abimelech sat heavily on his throne. "You almost caused God to destroy me and my family. I will send sheep to you, and menservants and maidservants. Take your wife and go."

"May we continue to live within your lands?" Abraham asked.

"You know my land. Dwell where you would like. It is yours."

He moved to stand in front of me. "I have given your brother a thousand pieces of silver to cover the sins I committed against you. Please accept this to atone for my misdeeds."

I nodded, unable to speak, for my stomach struggled to remain stable. Abraham bowed to Abimelech and led me from his chambers.

When we returned to the privacy of our tent, I confronted Abraham. "Why did you not tell me Terah is my father, too? It would have been easier to say you are my brother. I struggled to speak the words, because I thought it a lie."

"Did you not know?"

"I lived with my mother and father when we married."

"Eliora married Tomer after your birth. You were still small. Mother and Eliora did not live well together in Father's home. Father was overbearing, insisting on things Eliora refused to do. I heard the arguments even from my rooms, they were so loud. When Eliora left our home with you, I cried. I loved you even then."

"You loved me as a baby, and you still love me?" Warmth filled my chest.

"I will always love you." He hesitantly took my hand in his. "I have wanted no one else as my wife but you."

I stepped into his arms and he held me close. "I have loved you since I could remember. I did not know you were my brother."

"Eliora did not tell you?"

"The only father I ever knew was Tomer. He was gentle and kind to me and my brothers and sisters. I loved him," I murmured as Abraham stroked my hair.

"He was good to you. Better than Terah was."

I leaned back in Abraham's arms to see his face. "Terah had his good times with us."

He grimaced. "Then he gave me to the priests of Elkenah as a sacrifice."

"He did that. Can you forgive him?"

He pulled me back into his arms. "I forgive him, because I must as a follower of Jehovah. Besides, he gave you to me. He insisted that Tomer and Eliora visit often."

"We did that."

I leaned against his chest until my stomach revolted. I rushed out the tent door.

Abraham followed me and watched with some consternation as I lost the food I had eaten when we returned from Abimelech's home.

"Are you ill?" he asked, handing me a cup of water to cleanse my mouth as I wiped the nastiness away from my mouth.

I nodded.

"Have you been ill for long?"

"The last few days."

He touched my forehead. "You do not burn."

"No. I will not. Can you not guess my problem?"

He gazed at me like a little boy before his father with no answers and gently shook his head.

"I am with child." I smiled slightly. "Our visitors were correct. But I do not know how this happened."

Abraham chuckled. "You know what we did."

I giggled with him. "Yes, I know what we did. But we are ancient. How did our bodies perform like young ones?"

"You know the answer to that as well." He looked leeringly into my eyes.

"Jehovah. Nothing is impossible for Him."

"Exactly."

"We should pray for Abimelech and his household," Abraham said. "He took you as his wife, believing you would be the one to give him a child."

"Sadiqe was excited that I am with child. None of the women in their household have been able to conceive in many years."

"Jehovah has closed their wombs fast. Let us pray for Abimelech and his women."

We moved inside our tent and knelt together to pray. He begged Jehovah to open the wombs of the women in Abimelech's household. He reminded Jehovah that Abimelech had not touched me and had done all he could to redeem his mistake.

Over the next days, Abraham searched the land of Gerar until he found Mamre, a plain large enough to support all our animals. We moved our household, all our people and all our animals there, setting up our tents once more to create a small village. Others moved my possessions and set up our tent for me, for which I was immensely grateful. Between my rebelling stomach and concern for my growing child, I was careful to do nothing requiring heavy lifting.

We received news within two months that Sadiqe was with child. Jehovah had heard our prayers.

Chapter Twenty-One

Nothing is Impossible

Carrying Isaac was easier than I expected. Abraham insisted I rest often and do less work. Because Hagar was kept busy with Ishmael, he called on Yael's daughter, Liora, to serve me, so I would not overdo. We both remembered that fearsome day when I lost the only other child that had settled within my body.

Finally, three months after we settled in living in Mamre, the messenger Abraham sent to search for Lot in Sodom and Gomorrah returned.

Abraham settled him in front of the tent and invited me to join them. He asked Liora to serve us cakes and wine. While we ate, the man told us what he had learned.

"As we journeyed toward Sodom and Gomorrah, the land grew more desolate than we remembered."

"It is along the Jordan River and greener than the plain," I said.

"Nothing grows in that desert land anymore. We did not even see any lizards or mice, nor serpents or wolves. The land is barren where those two cities once were."

"It was the greenest land," I said.

"I remember it was green, but not now. It is drier than any place I have ever been." The messenger shook his head. "No bricks remain. Nothing that would suggest that cities once stood there. I only know they once did because it is the right place."

"And Lot?" Abraham asked. "Did you find Lot?"

The messenger inhaled deeply. "Eventually. The small city of Zoar still stands in the mountains. I went there, asking about Lot. One man spoke to me about his memories of Lot on the day of the immense fire. Men who ran to the walls of Zoar to see what had happened lost their sight. Some blame Lot for coming to them. Others say he protected them from the terrible fire, for Jehovah loves Lot."

Abraham agreed. "Jehovah does love Lot. Perhaps Zoar was not destroyed because they took Lot in."

"What about Galya? Did the one who saw Lot see Galya?" I asked.

The messenger closed his eyes and shook his head. "No one in Zoar saw her. Lot had his two youngest daughters with him. They left Zoar soon after the dust and smoke settled."

"No Galya?" I asked.

He shook his head. "After searching for many days, I finally found him hiding in the mountains with his youngest two daughters."

"But Galya? What about Galya?" I asked.

"His wife is no more."

"What happened?" I cried. *How could Galya be no more? A beautiful, vivacious woman. I hoped to see her again.*

Abraham took my hand. "Give him time to tell you." He turned to the messenger. "Did Lot tell you what happened?"

"It took much convincing. He did not want to speak of it. He shuddered as he spoke. He had not cleaned himself for many days." The messenger wrinkled his nose.

"What did he tell you?" Abraham asked.

"He had visitors the night before the fire. Three holy men came to Sodom. He tried to keep them out of the city, but they insisted on entering. He took them into his home and locked the door."

I glanced at Abraham. *It must have been the visitors who came to us.*

"Lot made a feast for them and all was well, until the men of the city surrounded the house, seeking the visitors."

The messenger took a sip of his wine and took his time swallowing it. Abraham and I waited.

"They banged on the door and windows, calling to him to bring his visitors out. They wanted to know the visitors, as they knew all the other men in the city."

I cringed and swallowed the bile that had risen in my throat. *They wanted that for the holy men? Sick.* Abraham squeezed my hand.

"How can a city be so vile to demand that of holy men?" The messenger shuddered. "Lot offered his two younger daughters, virgins, to them, but they would not take them. They wanted the holy men and pressed on him, almost breaking his door. The mob would have crushed Lot, but one of the holy men opened the door enough to pull him inside."

My heart raced at the thought of those men taking Lot's daughters. *How could he offer them? How could he give the visitors to the men of Sodom?*

The messenger took another sip of wine and continued. "When the men of Sodom would not stop beating on Lot's house, the holy men cursed them. The wicked men could no longer see to find the door."

"Did they escape then?" I asked.

The messenger shook his head. "The visitors asked Lot if he had other family, sons or sons-in-law and married daughters. The visitors called on him to bring all his family to his home. He went into the city and begged his sons and married daughters to join him in his home where it would be safe, but none would believe him."

"They have forgotten Jehovah and His love," Abraham murmured, rubbing his heart.

"They must have, for they refused to leave their homes and the wickedness in the city," the messenger said. "Somehow, the holy visitors helped Lot, his wife, and daughters to escape the city. They were told to flee to the mountains and not look back. Lot argued with the visitor, fearing he could not live in the mountains. Instead, he convinced the visitor to allow him to go to Zoar, which was not as wicked."

"Lot always wanted to do things his way," I mumbled, holding my arms across my stomach.

"And I tried to bargain for Lot's safety, too, begging for their protection if they could find as few as ten righteous men. Obviously, they could not."

"Only one, Lot, would leave Sodom. They destroyed all the rest in the fire. Lot hurried with his daughters to Zoar."

"What happened to Galya?" I asked, dizziness causing me to grab at Abraham's arm for support.

"She turned to look back..."

"And?" Abraham and I asked in unison.

"One daughter was behind her and saw it. She turned back toward Sodom and ..." the messenger swallowed and took a sip of wine. "She became a pillar of salt."

My heart pounded in my ears. "For disobedience?" I gasped.

The messenger lifted a shoulder. "That is what the daughter told me."

"More than disobedience," Abraham said, his voice shaky. "She must have longed for the life in the city, must have wanted to return to the life she had there. Jehovah would not have punished her so intensely otherwise."

"She will be a warning to others for centuries," I whispered.

"She will. We must look forward to the wonderful things Jehovah has for us, not to the enticements of the world." Abraham frowned into the distance, as if seeing the pillar of salt that once was Galya.

※※※※

Everyone in Mamre soon became aware that I would soon have a child. At first, the women feigned disinterest, to avoid embarrassing me, in my old age. As my body grew larger, I could not deny it and the women finally asked me about it.

"Are you not well past the years of giving birth?" Bara asked one afternoon when we worked together to dye wool.

I touched my stomach where the child kicked. *A child for me in my old age. His kicks are strong and he is healthy.* "I am, many years past that time."

"How is it possible that you are now with child?"

"Jehovah has made it so. I laughed when holy visitors came to tell us I would have a child. Abraham and I are both old. I did not know how it could be. But with God, all things are possible."

"Truly so," Bara agreed. "Your child proves it to be the truth."

We dyed the wool a beautiful blue. Hagar helped me weave blankets, as I had helped her weave years before when she carried Ishmael. She and the other women of our household helped sew clothing for baby Isaac.

I enjoyed the experience of Isaac moving within me, although sometimes he kept me awake with his kicking. It amazed me to have him within me. Jehovah truly was good to me.

I spent many hours in prayers of thanksgiving.

Ishmael did not come near me often during the time I carried Isaac. I thought he stayed busy, helping Abraham, who took him with him when he tended the sheep. Ishmael soon learned all their names and walked with them to the pastures. I loved watching Ishmael and Abraham and wondered what Abraham would teach Isaac. I expected he would teach him about the animals. As the promised son, he would need to know about Jehovah. Abraham would teach him about sacrifices and other important rites.

Time passed quickly, and soon it was near the time for my child to be born. My body felt heavy and unwieldy. I looked forward to seeing my son. My thoughts turned to the day when Hagar delivered Ishmael. I remembered her screams and pain. Could I give birth without screaming and making myself look bad?

Before the time came, I talked to Abraham. "What can I do? I do not want to scream and be unseemly when it is time for Isaac to be born."

"All women suffer when their children are born," he said, taking me into his arms. My stomach had grown so big, we struggled to kiss.

"I have heard they do, and I understand it is the will of Jehovah that we suffer. I am willing to suffer the pain. I do not wish to be considered a fool."

"Because you react to intense pain as all women do?" He smiled at me in the way he had when we were newly married.

I grinned at him. "I do not want people to consider me a silly woman. Is there anything you can do for me?"

"Perhaps," he said. "I found a book recently among those I received from my fathers. It is one you should have."

"Why?"

"Eve wrote it. Perhaps it will give you an idea of how to suffer the pain of childbirth with dignity."

"Dignity?" I giggled. "I suppose I am being silly." He had put a word and meaning to my fears.

He chuckled. We had not laughed like this in many years. "There must be a way to maintain some of your dignity while giving birth?"

"Have you witnessed childbirth?" My giggles ended.

"Not human childbirth, but I have helped many animals — horses, cows, sheep, and goats. Even they suffer in birth."

"Do you think Eve said anything about the struggle and the pain?"

He lifted a shoulder. "Perhaps. It will give you something to do in these last days."

"Something to do? I have many last-minute details to finish."

"The other women will help with that. You need to rest to prepare for the birth." He walked to his desk and pulled a book from a shelf, one I had seen before, when I dusted, but had not opened. "Take some time to read this. Perhaps you will find something that will help you with the pain."

He handed the book to me. On the cover it simply said, "Eve."

I opened the book and read. It intrigued me. *Did this come from her, our first mother? I had heard of her, though with few details.* I hugged the book close, feeling her presence through the cover. Silly. I know.

I did not know the challenges that faced our first parents. I grieved when her children turned their backs on the truths their parents taught. Her solutions to challenges surprised me. So many were similar to what I might do.

Then I found it.

I took the answer to Abraham. "I found the solution to my problem," I said. "Here in Eve's book. Adam placed his hands on her head and prayed, giving her a blessing from Jehovah."

Abraham read the pages I had marked, nodding and humming as he read.

"What would you have me bless you with? I do not think I can ask Jehovah to take all the pain away."

"I do not want the pain taken away, for I desire to have the full experience of childbearing. I only desire that I can experience childbirth with grace."

Abraham nodded. "Let me take this to Jehovah."

I nodded and opened the book once more, reading the last pages of the book. As I finished, Abraham returned.

"Jehovah agrees," he said.

He stepped behind me and lay his hands on my head. His prayer spoke of the love Jehovah had for me, and his understanding of my apprehension when told I would give birth to a son.

At last, he spoke of my desire to deliver the child with grace. "Sarah, it is God's will that women's sorrows be multiplied in conception. You have sorrowed for many years. Though you will suffer as women suffer during this birth, you will endure with grace. Your child will be born strong and will grow to be a father of nations."

His words calmed the fear in my soul.

When I woke in the night a week later with cramping in my stomach, stronger than those I had felt when I lost my first child, I did not fear.

I reached out to Abraham. "It is time."

"Time?" he mumbled.

"The child ..." I grunted and breathed through another pain. "Your child wants to meet his father."

"Now? In the middle of the night?"

"Bara says most children choose to be born at night."

"And my child will be like most of the others." Abraham pulled himself up to the side of the bed.

I groaned with the next pain. They were coming close together. "I think you should get Bara."

"Bara? Oh, yes. I will go get her." He pulled a robe around him and rushed out of our tent. I offered a prayer begging for help between the pains.

Bara bustled into our tent with a basket of supplies.

"Time?" she asked.

I gritted my teeth and nodded. She busied herself making preparations. I did not see her preparations, for another the pain ripped through my body. I controlled it by breathing deeply and gripping the edges of the bed.

It took hours of intense pain that exhausted me more than ever before, but the child was finally born long after the sun rose, brightening the tent. I heard Bara slap his buttocks, then Isaac squalled.

He lived. I had a child. Abraham had a child born to me.

Thank you, Jehovah.

Bara cleaned the babe and wrapped him in a blanket Hagar had helped me weave before handing him to me. I held his warm, tiny body in my arms and inhaled his scent. Wonderful. My child. I did not expect this ever to happen. She showed me how to help him find my breast and nurse.

She then turned her attention to me, cleaning up the blood and mess of giving birth. At last, she opened our tent door and invited Abraham in to see his son.

He bent over and stroked Isaac's little face with a soft finger. He then gazed into my eyes.

"I wanted to laugh that day, too," he whispered. "I wondered how an old couple like us, long past the time of raising a family, could ever have children." He bent over and kissed me gently. "And now we have a son."

"Isaac, as the visitor promised."

"Yes, Isaac. We laughed at the thought. Now we will laugh as he grows."

The child stopped eating and I gently lifted him upward. "Do you want to hold him? Do you remember how?"

"I remember." He sank into a chair beside me and lifted Isaac from my arms.

I lay back on the bed, watching him speak low and soft. "Your name is Isaac because your mother and I laughed. We struggled to believe such old people would have their first child. You are loved, Isaac, my beautiful child."

Chapter Twenty-Two

Banished

On Isaac's eighth day, Abraham took him from my arms and took him out to circumcise him for all those in our household to see. I stayed in my bed, grateful I did not have to participate in that rite.

The day after I rose from my bed after Isaac's birth clean from the effects of his birth, the three visitors who announced our son's birth returned. Abraham welcomed them to sit in front of our tent in the shade.

I stayed inside nursing Isaac, listening to them. Abraham asked them about Lot.

"He is well, although his daughters have forgotten the laws of God. They got him drunk and now both of them will soon give birth to a child fathered by him. There were other men in the world, men who love Jehovah. They should have waited."

I covered my mouth to avoid being heard by our visitors. They were right. My heart beat wildly, remembering my laughter.

"What happened?" Abraham asked.

"They believed they were the last ones left on the earth, even though they left Zoar and all the men living there. They gave their father wine until he was drunk, then enticed him."

I shook my head. How could those young women be so faithless?

"But we are not here to report on Lot. Your man shared the story with you. We are here to meet your child, Isaac."

Abraham came into the tent. "They want to meet our son."

"And Sarah should come out as well," one of them called.

Abraham took Isaac and helped me to stand. "Come outside with me."

We stepped through the tent door where the three visitors waited. The sun shone on them in a way that they glowed. When I looked for the sun, it did not shine on them. The light came from within them.

I fell at their feet.

One took me by the hand and lifted me up. "We are your servants. Worship Jehovah only."

I gazed into his beautiful face and saw only love. "You promised me a child a year ago."

"We did."

I took Isaac from his father's arms. "And look. Here is the child, Isaac, you promised." My child opened his eyes and smiled at them with a soft coo.

The visitors touched his face, his hands, his little feet, and expressed joy.

"He is beautiful as we expected," one said.

"Will you laugh when Jehovah promises you blessings again?" another asked.

I bowed my head and allowed tears of joy to drip onto Isaac's blanket. "No. I know now nothing is impossible for Jehovah."

"Remember this. Tell your family so they will remember. Nothing is impossible. Jehovah can do anything he chooses."

I bowed my head.

"Join us," one said.

I held with Isaac, who slept in my arms, listening to the men talk. Liora brought us sweet meat and cheese and wine.

"Why was Galya turned to salt?" I asked.

"Lot's wife had spent many years with her tent facing Sodom until at last they moved into the city. They partook of the city life."

"Not the wickedness?" I said with a gasp.

"She wondered about it, she watched it, it enticed her. She had family who stayed there, who refused to believe. We warned her she could not turn back, could not look back on the wickedness, not even hoping to see her children. The fire was too dangerous. It burned her."

"She could not have a second chance?" I asked through my grief. My memories of the time we spent together brought me to tears. I thought of our race to be prepared the first day of our travels, and holding her daughter shortly after her birth.

"This time, there were no second chances." The visitor wept with me.

When they left, I knew Galya would be remembered as a witness to the destruction that happens when we look back, desiring wickedness. I hoped to be remembered as one who trusted Jehovah.

In the months since Isaac's birth, Ishmael had little to do with his brother. Instead, he had stomped through the camp, giving orders to the herders and often making a nuisance of himself. He had become a self-centered braggart. Hagar did all she could to squelch his behavior, but the boy was stubborn.

When I said anything to Abraham about Ishmael, he shook his head and mumbled something about the ways boys behaved at that age.

"I would not know," I retorted. "I have never been a boy of nearly fifteen years, nor have I been the mother of one."

"It has been many years for me, but boys have not changed so much in all these years."

"Hagar should control him better. She allows him to run wild."

"He is my son as well," Abraham said. "I should be more strict with the lad."

"Lad? He is almost fifteen. He is a young man."

"Halfway there, I suppose."

"He is old enough to go with the herders and order them around."

"I have heard him do that," Abraham said. "I will talk to him."

Later, I overheard Hagar speaking to Ishmael. "You will be the father of many nations."

"I know," Ishmael said with a sneer. "I will be wealthy. Father is ancient already, and as his first-born son, his wealth will come to me."

"Sarah's son will inherit. He is the oldest son of his first wife."

"But I am the first son. I will get more and have the power over the people in our community."

I shook my head. Hagar still supported us, but I did not like to hear Ishmael speak that way. Jehovah had promised and given us a child. If Ishmael was to the one who inherited from Abraham, why would Jehovah insist that I have a child in my ancient years?

As Isaac grew older, Ishmael's comments grew more bitter, more difficult to listen to.

"As old Sarah sent my mother away when she carried me, I will send Isaac away when Father dies and I am the master," I heard him tell the boys his age.

"Old Sarah is too wrinkled and old to be a mother. I feel sorry for little Isaac," he said another day while boasting among the herders. "Worse for him, he will become a herder for me as the second son."

I inhaled deeply and kept my silence. I recognized it as rude boy talk. Through the years, other boys used bragging words similar to this, as they searched for their place among men, not knowing I heard them.

As had become the tradition, Abraham gave a feast for all who lived in our household and for all who lived close on the day when we would wean Isaac. He had ordered sheep and oxen slaughtered. Preparations kept the women busy for a week, baking cakes and breads and preparing other dishes.

On the day of the feast, Isaac would drink milk from a cup and enjoy many of the foods we ate. One part of me was happy, for the boy had grown big. He held me down during his feedings. But part of me wanted to cry. Isaac was all mine while I fed him. Now he would leave my breast and my side and move into the world of men. Not today, but soon.

Joy filled Abraham. He had two sons to carry on for him. Two sons who would be righteous and follow Jehovah. He carried Isaac on his shoulders to supervise the men who cooked the meat.

"Abraham is happy today," Bara said.

"He is," I said.

"He was filled with joy when Hagar gave birth to Ishmael and has had many happy days since then." Bara's eyes searched the area for Hagar. "She has been an excellent mother."

"Much too lenient, I fear," I said.

Bara's eyebrows dragged together. "Mothers are lenient with their sons. How is she any different?"

"Ishmael stomps around the camp with his chest puffed out, proclaiming his worth. He believes himself to be better than everyone here, even his father."

"I have heard him say those things. But look at Abraham with your Isaac. Abraham loves the little lad."

I followed Abraham as he bounced through the camp with Isaac on his shoulders. How did he have the strength to carry the child like that? He was a hundred years old. But Isaac seemed to cause him to remember his youth, even more than Ishmael had.

I hated the comparison. Isaac and Ishmael were both Abraham's sons. Jehovah gave both boys to him to raise up a righteous nation. Would Ishmael be righteous? He often made faces at his father during prayers and mocked him during sacrifices.

I sighed. Ishmael was Abraham's son.

As we feasted, Ishmael lounged at another table with the other boys, laughing and shouting.

"I hope Isaac enjoyed nursing from his mother. He will not have her to protect him anymore. He will have to grow up and learn how to be subject to me, his older brother. I will inherit. Isaac will get my leftovers as I give my scraps to the dogs." Ishmael tossed fat from his meat to the dogs.

Scraps? For my son?

"He will wish he still nursed at his mother's teat," Ishmael continued.

"That is enough!" I said, rising to my feet. My stomach hardened and my jaws hurt from clenching my teeth. "Isaac will not be your slave. He is Abraham's son."

It surprised me when I spoke so loudly, but as the words filled my mouth, all the anger returned from Ishmael's venomous words.

"Ishmael," Abraham bellowed. "You will apologize to your Aunt Sarah."

Ishmael pushed his chair back and leapt to his feet, the chair toppling over from his furious push. He turned toward me and opened his mouth. Nothing came out. He turned on his heel and ran away. I did not watch him run.

I slumped in my seat, heat rising from me. I would not allow Hagar's self-centered, rude, mocking son to take the birthright from my Isaac.

After a stunned silence, the guests began to eat and talk once more. I grit my teeth and stared at my plate, trying not to look at the others who joined us at the table. Eventually, the other women enticed me to join in the joy as they noticed all that Isaac ate from the table.

Later that night, after all our guests were gone, and we were in bed together again, I shared my grief with Abraham.

"I cannot believe the things Ishmael says about me and Isaac. Did you not hear?"

Abraham grunted. "I heard. And everyone heard your words."

"Abraham, it is time. Cast out that bondwoman and her son. He has mocked you and our son for the last time. That child of a bondwoman will not be heir with Isaac. He threatens to enslave him."

Abraham eyed the tent roof. "I cannot cast them out. Ishmael is my son."

"And when you die, will you allow the son given to us by Jehovah to become a slave to Ishmael because he is also your son?"

Abraham threw off the blankets and rose stiffly. "I must consider this. I will return." He pulled his robe over his sleeping robe and stalked out of the tent.

I thought of all the mockery heaped on me and Isaac by Ishmael. Each word he had said filled me with ire. *What had I been thinking to give Abraham my maid? I knew she wanted a family and would do everything for her child. Would I do the same thing in her place? Her pride emerged before Ishmael's birth. It would appear again.*

I formed all the arguments I thought I would need to convince Abraham when he returned. I could not have Isaac become a slave to that mockery of a son.

By the time Abraham returned to the tent, I had drowsed to a half sleep.

"It is done," Abraham said.

"Done?" I asked, still groggy. "What is done?"

"Jehovah told me to listen to you. Isaac is to be a father of many nations. He is the promised son. I have told Hagar that she and Ishmael must be gone before sunset tomorrow."

Suddenly wide awake, I swallowed all the arguments I had prepared. He had listened to me. Jehovah agreed with me. "Tomorrow?"

"Is that not soon enough? I can demand they leave tonight."

"No. Tomorrow is soon enough."

Abraham reached for me when he climbed back into bed. "Sarah, you are the love of my life. I love Ishmael as a son, but I will always do what you ask." He pulled me into his arms to kiss me.

Could I be wise in the things I asked? Would I repent of my demand that Ishmael and Hagar leave this time as I had before his birth?

Ishmael's words echoed in my head. "Isaac will wish he nursed at his mother's teat."

No. I would not repent of my decision this time.

Abraham rose early the next morning and took bread and a bottle of water to Hagar and Ishmael and sent them away. I watched from the door of our tent as she took Ishmael by the hand and walked away from the camp and into the wilderness.

Abraham had sacrificed a son for me, for my son.

Chapter Twenty-Three

Treaty

In the years that followed, we had peace. Isaac grew and all in our household loved him. He knew of our love and knew his place. He had no need to brag and push others around.

The herders took him into the hills with them to feed the animals when he grew big and strong enough, as they had taken Ishmael.

One day, he raced into our tent. "Mama, Mama," he cried.

"I am here. What do you need?" I said from my bed where I rested.

"You will never believe what I saw today. Three vultures circled over our heads. I wanted to see what they watched, but Eliezer would not allow me to get close."

"It is good you listened to Eliezer. He wants you to stay safe."

"I know Mama, er, Mother."

I grinned. He was growing so fast, even his language had grown from that of a child to a young man.

"We climbed the hill and looked down. There at the bottom of the hill, a lion had killed an antelope. He lay beside the body, chewing on the flesh."

"Good thing you did not run to see what brought the vultures."

Isaac's face brightened. "I watched jackals try to take away his antelope. He roared at them and chased them away." He roared and pretended to chase away the jackals. "The vultures flew in lazy circles." He flapped his arms and walked in a circle imitating the birds.

"Did the vultures ever get any of the antelope?"

"We went back to the sheep before the lion left his meal, but before we left for home, the vultures dropped from the sky. Eliezer said it was their turn to eat."

"Jehovah sets an order in all things, even when it is time for the vultures to clean up the bones left by the lions."

Isaac plopped on the floor beside me. "Is there an order in people? Are some better than others, like Ishmael used to say?"

"Do you remember Ishmael?"

Isaac shrugged. "He is my brother. I have asked the herders about him."

I squatted on the edge of the bed so I could see him. "And what did they tell you?" I lifted my eyebrows.

"They talk of how he thought he was better than them because Father is his father, too. He bragged how everything father owns would be his." Isaac tilted his head to the side and pursed his lips. "How can that be if I am Father's son as well?"

"Ishmael had many great and wonderful plans, but he forgot to ask Jehovah if it was what He wanted. I think Ishmael forgot Jehovah," I said, rubbing his back.

"Jehovah is good. He would not allow my brother to put me in bondage. Would he?"

I shook my head. "Not now. He lives far away, and no longer has claim to any of your father's possessions. You are his heir. If you listen to your father and do as he says, Jehovah will bless you as he has blessed your father."

"I will have a son in my old age?"

I chuckled. "Perhaps. But you will have a son. You will be father to many nations. Jehovah has promised your father. If Abraham is to be father of many, you must also be father to many."

"I should have my children earlier than you and Papa, er, Father did. It is easier to play with a child when you are not one hundred years old."

I tipped my head back and laughed. "You are right about that, Isaac. Do your best to have those children before you are so old."

Abraham entered the tent and looked back and forth between Isaac and me. We both struggled to stifle our giggling.

"Isaac has decided he should have his children before he is one hundred. It will be easier to play with them."

Abraham's face crumpled in laughter as he joined us.

When Isaac left us to do his chores, Abraham leaned back in his chair. "I have made a treaty with Abimelech and Phichol."

I turned toward him with my lips parted and a tingling in the base of my neck. "Oh? What kind of pact would you make with them?"

Abraham rubbed his eyes. "They see God is with me. They wanted me to swear that I would not deal falsely with them or with Abimelech's sons."

"That sounds like a simple thing to swear. You would not treat them poorly, even without the treaty."

"That is why I agreed. But Abimelech needed to know about his servants."

"What have they been doing?" I moved behind him and massaged his shoulders.

"Ah. That feels so good." He lifted his shoulders and relaxed them. "Abimelech's servants fought against ours and took the well we dug."

"No! Were any of our men injured?" My fingers stopped moving on his shoulders.

"Bruised and battered, but no serious injuries. But it hurts to lose that well. Our animals need it to survive."

"What did Abimelech do?" I returned to massaging Abraham's head and shoulders.

"He did not know what his servants had done. He promised it would never happen again." He tipped his head back and closed his eyes. "I cut out seven ewe lambs and took them to him. He asked why I had done this."

"Why seven ewes? Does he not have enough sheep already?"

"He asked the same thing, but I gave it to him as a witness that the well was mine, since I and my people had dug it."

"And did he accept them from you?" I asked, allowing my fingers to move along the edges of his eyes.

"He did. We made a covenant to treat each other fairly and not take from each other or our sons what belongs to the other."

"So your son is part of this? Does Isaac know?"

Abraham lifted his head. "Not yet. I must tell him." He took my hand and kissed it. "Thank you for listening."

He strode from the tent, calling for Isaac.

"Yes, Father," Isaac's youthful voice echoed into the tent.

"Come, I have something to show you."

Their voices drifted away. I relaxed for a moment before rising to go help Liora with dinner.

Isaac continued to grow. He soon stood almost as tall as Abraham. Not only did he have a tall, strong body, he listened to his father's teachings. Each day, his faith in Jehovah grew.

And Isaac learned about other parts of his father's life. He went with Abraham into the hills to feed and water the animals. Soon, he could lead the sheep to green pastures and gently flowing streams.

He went with Abraham into the city to sell the wool and met many of the kings and leaders of the land surrounding our home camp.

"Mother, the women are beautiful in Gerar. Do you think there is one there for me? One as beautiful as you?" he asked one day after returning from the city with his father. "King Abimelech told me of the time he wanted you to be his wife. Why did you say you were Father's sister?"

"He asked me to say that." I kept my hands still in my lap. "Your father has had experiences when men would take his life if I they knew I was his wife. And I am his sister. His father, Terah, is also my father. Our mothers are different, and I lived with Tomer as a father, since my mother left Terah."

"You are brother and sister?" Isaac yelped.

"It happens, still, although not as often as it did in earlier days. When our fathers left the ark, there were only brothers and sisters and cousins to marry.

When Eve and Adam first populated the earth, their children had no others to marry, only their brothers or sisters."

"I have not thought about that," he said, shuffling his feet. "Who will I marry? I have no sisters. The women in the surrounding lands do not believe in Jehovah. Father has taught we should marry within the faith."

"It is best, for a wife who believes in one of the gods of their land will entice you to follow her gods. How many of them believe they should sacrifice children to their gods?"

Isaac dropped his head. "Every one I have heard of sacrifices their children. How can they do that?"

I shook my head. "I have no way to understand that. But be careful. Do not get close to those women. You do not want to lose your soul to one of them."

Later, Isaac made friends with the son of Abimelech, who was born shortly after Isaac. As good friends, they visited together whenever their fathers met.

"Mother, Parviv suggested I should spend some time with his sister, Fariba. She is a lovely girl."

"But she follows El, does she not?"

"Yes. And El insists on the sacrifice of children. I cannot ..."

Over the next years, Isaac came to me often with this concern. "Who will I marry?"

It concerned me as well. Who would he marry? He had passed the age of marriage, and had not found a wife.

One night when Isaac was older, after he had asked me the question yet again, I brought the question to Abraham. "Who will Isaac marry?"

"He cannot marry a Canaanite," he said, drawing back. "They worship gods—"

"—who sacrifice children. None worship Jehovah. I know. Who will he marry? He has questioned me about this many times."

"And he has asked me the same thing. I have sent a messenger back to Harran. I hope Nahor and Milcah have a daughter."

"But their daughter would be older. Isaac was born in our later years."

"Perhaps a granddaughter, or a daughter of their old age. I have sent to see if they still follow Jehovah and if they have daughters."

"Have you mentioned this to Isaac?"

Abraham shook his head. "I do not want him to plan on a wife from Harran. Until I know, I will keep it to myself."

"And to me."

Abraham smiled. "Yes. It is for us to know. Isaac will learn soon enough. But he has promised me he will not take a wife from among the Canaanites nor the Egyptians."

"It is no wonder he asks me so often who he will marry."

Chapter Twenty-Four

Another Sacrifice

Age began to restrict my movement. I could no longer stride across our camp without stopping to rest and breathe. My lungs hurt from the effort to move. Added to that, pain would clench my heart. I moved slower and did less work. Each day, I thanked Jehovah for the girl who helped me with our home.

One day, when Isaac was an older lad and age had bent me low, Abraham came to me.

"Jehovah has commanded me to go to Mount Moriah to offer a sacrifice." He set his open hand against his heart, then sunk into a chair beside me.

"That is a long way to go to sacrifice. Is it not possible to sacrifice at your altar here?"

"It is Jehovah's command that we go to the land of Moriah. I am to take Isaac..." His voice weakened. He cleared his throat. "... take Isaac with me."

"You will both leave me?" My body trembled unexpectedly at the thought. "I fear for you to travel such a distance."

"I am strong. I can do it. It is you I fear for," Abraham said. "You are not as strong as you once were, but you are still as beautiful."

I swatted at his arm playfully. "At this age, living is beautiful."

He bent over to kiss me. "I have asked Danil and Bara to watch over you while we are gone."

"Danil is almost as old as you, and Bara is almost as old as me."

"True, but Danil and Bara have Eliezer and his wife to help care for you if needed. They will all keep you company while I am gone. Do not fear. I will not be gone long."

"It is many days to Moriah. When will you leave?"

"We leave at sunrise tomorrow morning. We will return as soon as we can after the sacrifice."

"You and Isaac are not going alone, are you? It is not safe, and it is far for you to walk."

"No. I am taking two young men and riding on my donkey. I am too old to walk to Moriah."

"Promise me you will take care of Isaac and yourself? I would be bereft without you."

Abraham swallowed. "I promise. We will return as soon as we can."

Early the next morning, Abraham gently kissed me goodbye. "We are off."

Isaac came to where I watched from the tent door and kissed me on the cheek. "Do not worry, Mother. I will take care of Father."

"You do that, son. Come home safely to me."

I watched them ride away. As they rode over the hill, I saw what had been quietly bothering me. They took no wood on the back of the donkey, and no lamb for the sacrifice. They could cut wood, but what would Abraham sacrifice? What would he sacrifice?

I thought about our discussion. He had not inspired joy or confidence. Why no lamb? Then I understood.

I returned to my bed and lay with tears dripping into my ears. Would Jehovah demand Isaac as the sacrifice?

Later, I wiped my tears and rose from my bed. I went to my loom, determined to weave a blanket for Isaac. He would need to marry in the coming years. I would provide a robe for his marriage made in the colors of our desert.

Liora brought me food, and I ate it beside the loom. I stayed at the loom much of the day for the week that Abraham and Isaac were gone. Each time the shuttle moved, I prayed Jehovah would protect my son and my husband. Each time I tamped the threads close, I begged for their safe return. "Do not take my son, my only son, as sacrifice," I prayed. "But if you must take him, I will submit to your will."

I only left the loom to eat and sleep. Sometimes, during the day, I would drowse next to my loom, but I did not leave it.

"You must rest," Liora said each day. "You are not as young as you once were."

"I know, but if Isaac is to have a marriage robe, I must make it now. I will not be here forever."

After four days, I walked to the tent door each day to stare down the trail leading toward Moriah. Where were Abraham and Isaac? On the eighth day, the fabric on the loom was nearly complete. I stretched and walked to the doorway of the tent and frowned down the road toward Moriah. My men should return soon.

When no men crossed the hill toward home after an hour, I returned to my loom. I wanted to have the fabric made for Isaac's robe. Surely Jehovah would bring him home to me.

I allowed tears to drip down my face as I finished my weaving. It was done. I could make a marriage robe for my Isaac. As I tied off each thread, I prayed Jehovah would bring them home to me.

I had tied all but one thread off when I heard a shout of welcome from outside. Liora rushed into the tent.

"Mistress," she cried. "You must come. They have returned." She helped me stand and I shuffled to the tent door.

Abraham rode on the donkey. Isaac strode beside him. The two young men strode behind. But my eyes were on my men. Jehovah had brought them home. I fell to my knees and thanked Jehovah for their safe return.

Isaac saw me kneeling in the doorway and ran to lift me. "Mother, are you well?" he asked.

"I am well. You are here with me. I am thanking Jehovah for your return."

The two young men helped Abraham off the donkey and he hurried to our side.

"All is well, my Sarah. I promised I would return with our son."

I trembled in their arms. "But you took no wood and no lamb. What did you sacrifice?"

"Later, when we have settled from our journey, I will tell you."

When Abraham and Isaac had put away their clothes and other possessions they took with them, they sat with me in our tent.

"You did not tell me what you sacrificed," I said. "I saw you did not take a lamb with you."

"I saw that, too," Isaac said. "I was so proud to be invited to join Father on this special sacrificial journey. Still, I wondered about it as we traveled. When I asked Father, he would only say that Jehovah would provide."

"And did He?" I asked with raised eyebrows.

Isaac cleared his throat. "Eventually. After a three-day journey, Father saw the place he searched for. He told the young men to wait for us. I carried the wood we had cut on the way and Father carried the fire and the sacrificial knife."

"You could not carry everything," Abraham said, leaning back in his chair.

"But we still did not have a sacrifice. And I asked Father again, 'Where is the sacrifice?' Once again, he told me Jehovah would provide." Isaac ran his hands through his sandy blond hair. "I carried the wood, Father carried the fire and the knife, but there was no lamb to sacrifice. Father insisted Jehovah would provide."

"And He did," Abraham said, biting his lip.

"Yes, but not as I expected," Isaac said, swallowing twice before he could speak again. "When we reached the place of sacrifice, I helped to build the altar from the stone we gathered near the top of the hill, and we set the wood on the altar." He swallowed again. "I asked a last time where we would find our lamb."

As I listened to this, my heart pounded in my chest, as though it would escape. Something was not right.

Isaac's voice dropped to a whisper and he rocked back and forth. "Father asked me to sit on the wood," he said, clutching his arms to his chest.

"No!" I cried. "You were the sacrifice?" A lump filled my throat.

"Jehovah had commanded that I take Isaac to Moriah and sacrifice him there," Abraham said. "I could not tell you before I left ... you would not have stayed here. It would have been dangerous for your health. I feared you would not be here when we returned."

"And what do you think I would have done if you had not brought my son home to me?" My voice lifted as the fear I had tamped down while they were gone, even as I had told Jehovah I would accept his judgments.

"He is here, all is well," Abraham said.

"He is here, but you set him on the altar. Did you lift the knife to slay him?"

Abraham dropped his eyes from mine with a moan. "I did."

"I could not believe my father would sacrifice me," Isaac said, breathing deeply.

"I have covenanted to obey Jehovah, no matter what he commands," Abraham whispered.

"But to sacrifice your son? After Terah gave you to the priests of Elkanah to be sacrificed?"

"I understood his fear. I saw the prayer on his lips as I prayed when the priests tried to sacrifice me. My heart filled my throat. My hands were so slippery with sweat, I struggled to hold the sacrificial knife. I did not want to sacrifice my son, the son of my old age, the only son the love of my life gave me." He gazed into my eyes, his eyes pleading for me to understand.

I closed my eyes. "What happened? How is it that my son sits here with us if Jehovah commanded you to sacrifice him?"

"I lay on the wood praying," Isaac said, his voice barely above a whisper, "when I heard a voice. I opened my eyes and saw an angel at the head of the altar."

"'Lay not your hand on the lad,' the angel said to me," Abraham murmured. "'Neither do any harm to him, for I know you fear the Lord your God, Jehovah, as you will withhold nothing from Him, not even your only son.'"

"But you still had no sacrifice," I said. My heart had skipped a beat and I let out the breath I held. "Did you sacrifice after all the effort you went through to get there?"

"I looked at our surroundings and saw a ram had caught his horns in a thicket. Sarah, it was not there when we arrived, for I looked." Tears flowed down Abraham's cheeks. "I walked all over the sacrificial site as we gathered rocks to build the altar. It was not there before, but there it was, a ram for the sacrifice."

Isaac blew out a big breath. "Father is correct. It was not there earlier. I gathered rocks from that thicket. But the ram was there. Father untied my bindings, and I helped him take the ram and tie it with the very bindings that had tied me." Tears now flowed freely down Isaac's face.

I gulped. Tears dripped from my face onto my dress. "And you sacrificed the ram?"

Abraham allowed a low sob to escape. "I did. As I told Isaac, Jehovah provided a sacrifice. I feared all the way to Moriah, even as I lifted the knife, I would be forced to sacrifice our son. It was difficult to see the ram for the tears of gratitude in my eyes."

"You brought my son home to me. I prayed from the moment I saw you leave without a lamb that Jehovah would not insist that you sacrifice Isaac. I spent my time weaving to keep from crying."

"And Mother," Isaac said. "You should have heard the words of the messenger. I will never forget the promise given to Father."

"You heard the voice?" Abraham asked.

"I did. He said that because you did not hold back even your son, your only son, Jehovah would bless you. He would multiply your seed, and you would have children to number greater than the stars in the heavens or the sand on the seashore. Your children would possess the gate of our enemies, and our children will bless all the nations. All because you obeyed the commandments of Jehovah."

The blessing had been repeated once more. If Isaac heard it, it would continue with him and his children. Jehovah be praised.

"I trusted Jehovah," Abraham said. "I know he can do anything. If he could fill your womb with a child many years after the time of women, Jehovah could have brought our son back to life. Nothing is impossible with Jehovah."

I rose and walked the short distance to Isaac and put my arms around him. "I am grateful Jehovah provided a ram, and I did not have to hear how He brought you back to life." Our tears mingled as we embraced.

Abraham joined us. "I prayed all the way there for Jehovah to provide another sacrifice. However, since I heard the angel speak to me there on the altar in Ur, I have devoted my life to obedience to Jehovah."

"I prayed for you with almost every breath from the moment you crossed the hill out of Mamre until I heard the shout that you had returned. Jehovah heard my prayer."

"And mine," Abraham and Isaac echoed.

In the days shortly after Abraham and Isaac returned from Moriah, the messenger returned from Harran. Abraham walked with him into the hills to hear the news of his brother and sister.

My health had declined, and I spent much of my time in bed. I read Eve's book and felt compelled to write the story of my life. Abraham brought me vellum and a pen so I could begin.

It has been difficult. I have developed a cough, and as I write I must stop to hack and catch my breath. It has caused this to take longer than I hoped.

Keturah is a lovely young woman who helps me each day. I appreciate all she does for me. She helped me complete the marriage robe for Isaac. I hope to live long enough to see him married.

Abraham came to my bed to share the news his messenger had brought to him from Harran. The news is good.

Milcah has born eight children to Nahor. One of these, Bethuel, has a daughter, Rebekah. Abraham hopes his cousin will allow her to marry Isaac. I pray he does, for the Canaanites do not worship Jehovah. Isaac must marry a believer.

I have told my story. All I can do now is lie here and wait for Jehovah to take me home.

Abraham is not able to take care of himself without a wife. I will suggest he take Keturah as his wife after I am gone. She is young. Perhaps she can give him more children than I did. Two is more. May Jehovah bless my good Abraham with more family after I am gone.

For all my grandchildren who read this, I must share my sorrow for being so small with Hagar. I gave her to Abraham. Ishmael is his son. I should not have driven them away. Perhaps Jehovah would have changed his temperament. Perhaps if Ishmael had lived with his father until old age, he would have loved Jehovah and learned to treat others with respect.

I repent for doubting Jehovah. If I have learned nothing else, I have learned that all things are possible with Him. If He could take a dry husk of an old woman like me and give me a child, He can do anything.

The coughing increases. I cannot write more.

I love you Isaac. Stay true to your faith in Jehovah. Serve Him well.

And, Abraham, you will always be my one true love. I will wait for you at Jehovah's feet.

Afterword

Women of the Covenant is a series I avoided for many years. I did not want to write something others have written. I don't like the competition. But my readers asked many times. At last, I conceded.

The stories of Sarah and Hagar intertwine. One cannot be told without the other. For that reason, I worked back and forth, writing Hagar's story and editing Sarah's story at the same time.

It was a challenge, but nothing like the last four will be. These will be the stories of Jacob's wives: Rachel, Leah, Bilhah, and Zilpah, stories of four women who lived together as wives and concubines of the same man. I am in no rush to tell those stories, but I will get to them soon.

As always, these books tell the stories of the women mentioned incidentally in the Bible. I endeavor to fill in the stories of their lives and share their courage and love.

Acknowledgements

Another book is written and you read it!

Thanks go to those readers who asked me to write this series. I fought writing this series telling the story of the wives of Abraham, Isaac, and Jacob for a few years. Others have written their stories. How could I compete? But my readers requested these stories. So, I did.

I must always thank my patient sweetheart, Jack, for his support. Some days I sat at my desk, others I sat beside him, often ignoring him, tapping my keyboard. Without his support, I would never get a book written.

My family always supports me. I am grateful for them. My mom and dad do all they can to help, and dad, who is now 95, is my final proofreader. Without my family's support, it would be much more difficult to write.

Another valuable support has been my ANWA (American Night Writers Association) support and sprinting groups. Writing as fast as I could for 30 minutes at a time got much of this book written. Thanks especially to Carol Malone.

As always, this would not be as good of a story without the efforts of my editor, Julia Allen. With her careful editing, this book is more readable for you. Additionally, the fantastic skills of Dar Albert, who has created another beautiful cover for this book. I give both ladies my heartfelt thanks.

My AngelCAST team read the final version and found the last typos and mistakes that needed to be fixed. Thank you, team!

Last, but never least, a big thank you, goes my reader, for choosing to read this book of fiction I spent my time writing. I would love to hear how you liked it.

Also By Angelique Conger

Ancient Matriarchs
Eve, First Matriarch
Into the Storms: Ganet, Wife of Seth
Finding Peace: Rebecca, Wife of Enos
Moving into Light: Zehira, Wife of Enoch
Out of Darkness: Imma, Wife of Noah
We Stood with Them: Other Wives of the Prophets

Lost Children of the Prophet
Lost Children of the Prophet
Captured Freedom
Abandoned Hope
Brotherly Havoc
Betrayed Trust
Convicted Deliverance
Trouble Escaped
Contrary Devotion
Impassioned Grief
Love Defied
Hidden Purpose
Concealed Innocence

Struggle for Limhah
Combating Cults
Fighting Foreign Armies
Defending Faith

Into Egypt
Before Egypt
Discovery
Settlement
Enemies

Women of the Covenant
Sarah, Mother of Nations
Hagar, Mother of Sorrows

About the Author

Many would consider Angelique Conger's books Christian focused, and they are because they focus on early events in the Bible. She writes of a people's beliefs in Jehovah. However, though she's read in much of the Bible and searched for more about these stories, there isn't much there. Her imagination fills in the missing information, which is most of it.

Angelique Conger discovered the wonders of writing books later in her life. Books, however, have always been important to her. As a little girl in a small town, she was given her own library card at the tender age of five, highly unusual in those days.

Angelique reads a book, or three at once, much of the time. She reads most genres of books and, until a few years ago, only toyed with writing them. Since beginning, she has spent many hours each day learning the craft of writing and editing.

Angelique lives in Southern Nevada with her husband, Siamese cat, Sparky, and their tuxedo cat, Spicy. She enjoys visits from her grandchildren and their parents.

Printed in Dunstable, United Kingdom